Frank Trollope

The Lawyer's Daughter

A Novel. Vol. 1

Frank Trollope

The Lawyer's Daughter
A Novel. Vol. 1

ISBN/EAN: 9783337045869

Printed in Europe, USA, Canada, Australia, Japan

Cover: Foto ©Andreas Hilbeck / pixelio.de

More available books at **www.hansebooks.com**

THE LAWYER'S DAUGHTER:

A Novel,

IN THREE VOLUMES.

BY

FRANK TROLLOPE,

AUTHOR OF

"BROKEN FETTERS," "THE MARKED MAN,"
"THE GLADSTONES," "AN OLD MAN'S SECRET."

VOL. I.

London:
CHARLES J. SKEET,
10, KING WILLIAM STREET, CHARING CROSS.

1878.

TO

MRS. EDWARD KOCH,

THESE VOLUMES

ARE

AFFECTIONATELY DEDICATED

BY

THE AUTHOR.

THE LAWYER'S DAUGHTER.

CHAPTER I.

On the western shores of the Gulf of Spezia, stood a handsome-looking villa commanding the entire scenery of what may be called the Lake of Spezia, so completely are its waters shut in from the oftentimes boisterous sea. The villa was on a slight elevation; the grounds around it were planted with flowering evergreens, and a well-kept lawn extended to the water's edge. It was protected from the north wind by a considerable plantation.

The house was only one storey in height, but it covered a considerable space. The interior fittings were simple, yet elegant. A verandah ran around three sides of the building, supported by pillars, the whole covered by thousands of blossoms of the sweet-smelling parasites that wound up them and crept along its roof.

The view from the villa was singularly picturesque and varied; directly opposite, embowered in masses of olive, orange, almond, and fig trees, was the town of Venere, and to the south-east rose that remarkable promontory, Cape Corvo. To the right, on the same shore, perched on abrupt and steep rocks, might be seen the Castle of Venere, a place of considerable importance, and strongly fortified. It defended the entrance to the Gulf. To the left, and distant half-a-league, was the town of Spezia, and, nearer still, a small monastery of Dominican monks, in which monastery was a very ancient and beautiful chapel.

At the period of our tale the villa was inhabited by an Italian lady, known as the Signora Erizzo, who, seventeen years before, had purchased and beautified it. Almost past the middle period of life, the Signora still retained every mark of having in her youth been

remarkably beautiful. She had for a companion a fine handsome boy of about five or
six years of age, who called her aunt. Her
household consisted of a very respectable
female attendant of her own age, and two
younger female domestics.

The Signora lived a very retired life, and
with the exception of Padre Geronimo, a monk
of the neighbouring monastery, she received
no visitors; but the poor and the afflicted
always found help, advice, and kindness on
application.

As Ferdinando grew in years, Padre Geronimo,
a man of sixty years or more, of dignified appearance, took him under his guidance, and
became greatly attached to him. At the age
of twelve, the Signora Erizzo wished him to be
placed in the Military College of Genoa, and
thither the Padre, obtaining permission from
his Superior, accompanied him. The boy was
at the College for five years, eclipsing his fellow-
collegians in almost all their studies, but more
particularly in all military exercises. Before

attaining the age of seventeen, his singular dexterity, combined with great strength, astonished the celebrated Professor of Fence in Genoa, the Signore Paulo Veroni, who boasted that, ere another year, his pupil would be a match for the best swordsman in Italy or France.

At this period the use of the sword, and especially the small sword, was in great repute throughout Europe; Masters of Fence travelling from Court to Court challenging and defying each other, and combats in theatres and before large assemblies of the people were openly practised. Sometimes, and indeed frequently, these combats were not merely trials of strength, but life wantonly sacrificed.

At the College, in Genoa, Ferdinando d'Erizzo formed a friendship with the younger son of the Marchese Durazzo, and, induced by him, he prevailed on his aunt, after much persuasion, to permit him to serve as a volunteer on board the same galley as the young Durazzo. Accordingly, at the age of eighteen, he sailed with the Genoese fleet, bound for the Levant, where war then raged.

In a saloon of the Villa Erizzo, as it was called, reposing on a couch drawn close to the window—for the month was May, and the hour the one preceding sunset—was the Signora Erizzo. The evening was lovely, and the air delicious ; the glories of the setting sun threw a charm of dazzling splendour over all around the villa ; the magnificent Gulf looking like a sheet of gold, for not even a ripple disturbed its surface, while the lofty towers and battlements of Castle Venere threw their deep shadows, in fine contrast, far over the placid waters.

Numbers of those picturesque craft of the Mediterranean—feluccas, zebecs, and others —lay listlessly on the water, neither disturbed nor moved by tide or wind ; while their crews were singing a favourite barcarole, which sounded sweetly in the still air.

Charming as was the scene before the eyes of the Signora Erizzo, her features wore a sad

expression; her once luxuriant hair had become white as snow, and the small thin hand
that lay resting on the couch, almost trans-
parent, the veins showing clear and distinct—
for, alas! the kind and good Signora was sinking fast, not from age, or from any of the
many maladies to which the human race is
subject, but gradually wearing out from the
effects of seventeen years of silent sorrow—
that sorrow which preys upon the heart in the
lone hours of night—that in spite of all our
efforts will occupy our thoughts even in our
daily occupations—eating into and corroding
the heart—sapping the foundations of life—
and slowly but surely bringing its victim to its
last resting-place on earth.

There was neither remorse, nor guilt, nor shame
to be traced on those once beautiful features,
but a close observer could occasionally see—by
the kindling of her dark and still fine eyes, by
the close pressure of the lip, and the firm closing of the small hands—that memory of the
past, the recollection of some terrible deed or

act, roused the slumbering energies of her once strong mind.

One of the Signora's hands rested on the couch, the other held a miniature, richly set in jewels and gold. Long did the invalid gaze upon the miniature, till her eyes grew moist and dim. She pressed it to her lips, to her heart, and then bent her aged head upon her hand and sobbed convulsively. The miniature was that of a female, richly habited in the remarkable costume of the Venetian dames of rank of the seventeenth century. It was a fair and exquisitely beautiful face, having a touch of sadness in the expression of the features. On her lap sat a child of about three years of age, the image of its mother.

The lady gazed upon this miniature long and earnestly ; the tears streaming down her cheeks, caused by the feelings struggling within her breast.

"Ah ! my God !" she murmured, "eighteen years of bitter sorrow, and the grave open before me, cannot obliterate or efface the one fearful hour that plunged me into a life of painful regret, and an undying desire for vengeance upon the man who caused all my misery, and who yet lives, glorying in his pride, in his sin, and in his security. But the day of retribution approaches," and lowering her head upon her wasted hands the sufferer wept bitterly.

Presently the door slowly opened, and the priest of the village, the monk of the neighbouring monastery, entered the saloon.

" Ah ! good Father," anxiously enquired the Signora, raising her head, " have you received any intelligence from Genoa. Has the fleet arrived ? "

" Not as yet, I fear, dear lady," returned the Padre, seating himself ; " but it is hourly expected, for a fast galley reached Genoa three days since with intelligence that it had sailed from Negrapont ; and no name in the list of those praised stands higher than that of Ferdinando d'Erizzo. It is reported that his great skill and courage saved the Admiral's galley from destruction."

"Ah! my noble boy!" cried the Signora, starting up, her eyes kindling for a moment with the fire of youth; but the next minute falling back from excessive weakness. "Alas! my good friend," she added, "I fear this poor weak frame will scarcely hold together till I clasp him to my heart."

"Nay, I trust and hope differently, Madam," observed the Padre.

"If it be God's will that I should not see him, my kind old friend," returned the Signora, after a minute's pause, "you are aware of everything I wish said and done. You know where all the documents and papers necessary to carry out my wishes are deposited."

"Yes, Signora," answered the Padre, "and all shall be attended to."

After remaining with the Signora in earnest conversation for some time, the priest retired, leaving the invalid to the care of the old and faithful attendant.

The next day the invalid was evidently weaker, though more free from pain, but ex-

ceedingly restless and anxious; the name of
Ferdinando constantly on her lips. The following morning she was unable to leave her
couch. Towards evening the rapid tramp of
a horse's feet was heard coming up the avenue
leading to the villa; and the next moment a
horse, panting and covered with foam, was
checked at the entrance door, and a tall, noble-
looking youth alighted—it was Ferdinando
Erizzo; who, with a beating heart and flushed
cheek, hurried to the invalid's chamber.

" My beloved son ! " exclaimed the dying
lady in a faint voice ; " the Almighty has heard
my prayer ! " and then feebly extending her
arms, they closed round the neck of the deeply
affected youth. He pressed his lips to hers ;
a faint murmur was heard—

" Bless you, my son !—Leave vengeance to
——." Her voice failed, and the next instant
the Signora Erizzo ceased to exist.

We pass over a period of ten or twelve days.
The mortal remains of the Signora Erizzo were
consigned to the grave ; and then it became

known that the name of Erizzo was an assumed one, and that Ferdinando had lost a
grandmother instead of an aunt.

Deeply and bitterly did Ferdinando d'Obizzi
(for such was the name he was entitled to bear)
bewail and mourn over the loss of one who
had been almost more than a mother to him.
He felt as if he had neither kindred nor tie.
He had always been aware that some mystery
existed with respect to her who he had from
childhood called aunt ; and he now felt a
feverish anxiety to unravel this mystery, whatever it might be.

Padre Geronimo was unceasing in his visits;
calmly and piously reasoning with and urging
his young friend to bend to the will of the
Almighty with resignation, and to look forward
with hope.   On one of these visits the Padre
said—

"My dear friend, it is time to show you a
memorial of the past, which will explain to you
fully and clearly the reasons that induced the
Countess d'Alberti to assume another name

and rear you, the heir of a noble family, in retirement and obscurity.   Come with me."

Ferdinando followed the Monk into the
chamber where his grandmother had breathed
her last sigh, and placing before him a handsome cabinet, presented him with two keys,
saying—

" Within that cabinet, my son, you will find
a drawer containing papers, deeds, and jewels.
In a small desk are two miniatures and a brief
memoir of the Countess's life which fully ex-
plains the past, and points out to you your
future career as far as human foresight can
do so."

The Padre paused for a minute and then
went on—

" I will now leave you ; after to-morrow I
will return, and we will then talk over that
which you will learn ; for all has been known
to me these many years.   Remember, my son,
whatever you see or read, a ruling Providence
watches over all.   Give not way either to rash
or intemperate vows or resolutions.   Curb the

demon of passion; kneel at the Throne of
Grace; humble yourself in prayer, and your
mind will become calm.   The happiness of
your future life depends, perhaps, on the events
of the next twenty-four hours—farewell."

For some time after the departure of the
Monk, Ferdinando stood like a statue; his
arms folded, his dark eyes fixed upon the
cabinet, but his thoughts far, far from the spot
on which he stood.   At length, with a strong
effort, he broke the spell that bound his
faculties.   With a deep sigh, murmuring half
aloud—

" Yes, kind friend, your advice is good and
pious; but I know—I feel—that some foul
wrong has been committed upon the departed
saint, who in life watched over my childhood
with all a fond mother's care.   If my surmise
be correct, and thou hast been wronged, I swear
I will avenge thee, even should I perish in
doing so."

He paused, pressed his hand upon his brow,
and for some minutes remained immovable.

His excitement calmed; he took the key, and unlocked the cabinet. It contained two large iron caskets, in each was a key, and conspicuously placed was a slip of parchment, on which was written—" This casket to be opened first by my beloved grandson, Ferdinando d'Obizzi."

" Grandson ! " repeated the youth in a thoughtful tone. " My mother's mother, no doubt."

With an anxious and beating heart, the young Marchese, without bestowing a thought upon the title thus suddenly revealed to him, opened the casket. Within it was another of cedar-wood. Raising the lid of the second he beheld a magnificent display of jewels; on these were placed two miniature cases. On one was a slip of paper, with merely the words —" *Your* beloved mother, *my beloved* child !"

Trembling with anxiety, he opened the case, and, with feelings scarcely possible to describe, he gazed upon the same lovely face which, a few days before, we mentioned as being held

in the hand of the departed lady whose real
name he now learned was Ellena, Countess
d'Alberti.

Tears came into the youth's eyes as he
looked with intense interest and love upon
those proud and beautiful eyes; proud only of
being the mother of the lovely boy she held
upon her lap.

"Oh! how beautiful! how very beautiful
was my mother!" murmured Ferdinando.

As he uttered these words many wild
thoughts and ideas rushed through his mind,
and a chill feeling crept over his frame. Long
and ardently he continued to gaze upon the
miniature, till it almost faded from his sight,
and then, with a sigh, he replaced it in the
case.

He took up the other case, expecting it contained the miniature of his father. As he
opened it, a slip of paper covered the inside.
The words he read on that paper drove all the
blood from his cheeks and lips. He stood
spellbound; his muscular arm stretched forth

as if grasping a foe. The perspiration ran from his head and face, while his dark eyes flashed with a feeling of terrible passion.

The words that caused this agony of mind were few, but fearful in their import. They were : —

"*The portrait of Bertran de Trevisano, Count of Brescia. The fiend in human form who cruelly murdered your ill-fated mother !*"

Ferdinando d'Obizzi, though very young, was a being of strong passions, and sudden and violent impulses; and yet of as kind and noble a nature as could exist in the human breast. No sooner were those words read than he fell upon his knees, and, with his dark, expressive eyes fixed on the miniature of his murdered parent, cried aloud—"Mother! dear mother, hear me! I swear by the Saviour of man—by all that is good and holy, if this fiend still exists—no matter where I meet him—in the court of kings—in the house of God—on the land or on the sea—I will slay him. Never will I wed, or dream of happiness, till he who murdered my mother dies by my hand !" and, bowing his head upon the casket, he remained silent and motionless for nearly an hour.

Reader ! the age of chivalry and wild vows had long passed at the period of our tale, still there remained a strong feeling of superstition and romance in the minds of the young Italian nobility. The murder of the Marchese d'Obizzi is, however, an historical fact, as is also the vow of the son. How the latter fulfilled his rash and inconsiderate oath, these pages will declare.

After a time the young Marchese arose from his knees, his face was pale as death, but his manner was calm and collected. With a steady hand he raised the miniature of his mother's destroyer and held it to the light ; gazing long and steadily, and sternly upon it. It was the likeness of a remarkably handsome man in the very vigour of youth ; dark complexioned, about two or three and twenty years of age, richly habited in the costume of a Venetian noble. His hair, raven black, was worn far back from a broad massive forehead, on which appeared a deep, narrow scar. The eyes, like the hair, were extremely dark; the chin remarkable from its massiveness.

"This is a face I will carry engraven on my heart and mind," murmured Ferdinando, as he put down the miniature and closed the casket.

The other casket contained deeds, parchments, and papers, all carefully tied and docketed; but the Marchese did not examine any of them. He was attracted by a scroll in the handwriting of his grandmother, on which was written—

"*The history of your ill-starr'd parent, my dearly-beloved grandson.*"

"For years, my child" continued the writer, "I existed only—living only on the hopes of vengeance. In you, Ferdinando, I reared, as I hoped—the avenger! Years rolled on. Age— though it did not blunt the memory of the terrible past—taught me that in my projects to crush sin, I was committing sin. Padre Geronimo, a good and pious monk, who once moved in the world high in rank, became my friend, my adviser, my comforter; and though the canker-worm still ate at my heart's core, yet I no longer felt the same all-devouring thirst for vengeance. You are now, child of my adored and never for a moment forgotten Ellena, arrived at years of discretion; read and judge for yourself, and may the Almighty, in His mercy, direct your heart and judgment.

" ELLENA D'ALBERTI."

Closing the windows of the chamber, and lighting the antique silver lamp that stood upon the table, the young Marchese d'Obizzi took the roll of paper, and seating himself close to the light, perused with an anxious and disturbed mind the brief history of his parents, which our readers will find in the next chapter.

CHAPTER II.

"My husband, the Count Jacomo d'Alberti, was a Venetian nobleman of high birth, considerable wealth, and one of the kindest and best of men. Of our four children, your unfortunate mother, Ellena, was the only one who lived beyond childhood, and, at the age of seventeen, married Ferdinando, Marchese d'Obizzi, considered one of the handsomest cavaliers in Venice. To my deep grief and dismay, I was left a widow shortly after the birth of Ellena. My whole happiness in life then became centred in her. She grew up surpassingly beautiful, and as innocent as she was lovely. I lived but in her presence. She was my earthly idol.

" Out of numerous suitors, your father was the favoured one. On their marriage I stipulated but for one thing—not to be separated

from my child. The Marchese made no objection, and we took up our abode in the
Palace Obizzi, situated on the Grand Canal,
and one of the most magnificent in Venice.

" I must now, painful to my feelings as it is,
speak of the wretch who destroyed all our
dreams of happiness. Amongst the disappointed suitors for the hand of my daughter
was a young nobleman, to whom, from the
very first, I took a strange and unaccountable
dislike, Bertran de Trevisano, Count of
Brescia, whose elder brother, the Marchese,
resided in Venice, holding high office under
the Government, and was moreover, exceedingly wealthy.

"The Count of Brescia was, at this period, in
his twenty-second or twenty-third year; handsome, accomplished, and considered the best
swordsman in Venice. He was madly in love
with Ellena; consequently his rage, when he
learned that the Marchese d'Obizzi was
preferred before him, knew no bounds. He
vowed the most deadly revenge, and, trusting

to his skill with the small sword, challenged the Marchese, having first grossly insulted him. He was, however, mistaken ; they fought, and the Count of Brescia received two wounds that confined him for nearly three months to his couch. On recovering, he retired to his estates near Brescia.

" Time rolled on, and you, my beloved grandchild, were born. Alas! how joyous we were. There appeared no cloud, even in the distance, to disturb our happiness !

" You were only three years old, when your father was roused from his dream of bliss by a summons from the Senate. The war in the Levant began, and your father was appointed to a high command, next to the Venetian Admiral. Need I describe the agony of the parting. Alas! your parents little thought it was for ever in this world.

" Now that I approach the fatal catastrophe that wrecked the peace and happiness of our family, my hand trembles and my heart throbs with agony. Oh, memory ! memory ! Seven-

teen years have not blotted out or erased the
bitter heartrending recollection of that hour.

" Some five months after the departure of the
Marchese for the Levant, I was roused from
my sleep by an appalling shriek. My chamber
was next to my daughter's. You slept in her
room, with your favourite attendant, a female
to whom your unfortunate mother was much
attached. I started up, appalled by that fearful shriek. It came from my daughter's
chamber. A lamp burnt in my room. Wild
with terror, I sprang from my bed, hastily put
on a shawl, and ran distracted, for cry after
cry came from my child's room. In my blind
eagerness and bewilderment I rushed to the
door, it flew open, and I fell into the chamber.

" This part of the palace was separated from
the chambers occupied by the male domestics.
Oh! merciful Providence! As I gained my
feet, I beheld my daughter in her night-dress
—her child screaming frantically—grasped
round the waist by a tall man. He turned
round as I arose from the floor, and by the

light of a lamp suspended from the ceiling I recognised Bertran de Trevisano.   With a dreadful imprecation he shouted, 'Die then, you and his cursed offspring!' and raising his stiletto, though I threw myself upon him, he plunged it into Ellena's bosom.   Twice did the monster strike, like an infuriated fiend!   I tore the child from his grasp; he struck at me; I shielded you, my grandson, with my body, and the blow felled me to the floor; I retained my senses for the moment, and just as he stooped to strike you, my dear boy, several male and female domestics rushed into the room and seized the monster.   The next instant I became insensible."

Ferdinando d'Obizzi paused; large drops of perspiration fell from his forehead, his face was fearfully pale, and a mortal agony seemed to paralyse the frame of the horror-stricken son of the ill-fated Ellena.   With clenched hands, his eyes—almost starting from their sockets—roamed over the dimly-lighted chamber as if they expected to encounter the shade of his murdered parent. Wiping the moisture from his forehead, he waited to regain composure, and then resumed.

"Oh! that return to life! To live over again the agony of that hour! My life! My joy! My child was dead! Never more were those fond and loving eyes to meet mine. Never more was that fond heart to beat with rapture as it used to do, when pressing you to her bosom. For weeks I was insane. I lost all control over my actions, and had to be watched night and day. At length a fever ensued, and, after two months of suffering, I became conscious of the past, and in a few days you were brought and placed in my arms. I vowed to live for you and vengeance.

"I now learned the doom the authorities of Venice pronounced upon the murderer. Bertran de Trevisano had been brought to trial. A plea of insanity was endeavoured to be proved from the period of his duel with your father. In vain our relations and friends asserted that this plea was a false one. He was, however, only condemned to ten years' imprisonment without confiscation of property.

"Misery and misfortune still pursued our unhappy family. Your father learned the fearful fate of his adored wife on the eve of a great naval engagement. Maddened by the intelligence, the next morning he rushed wildly and madly into the thickest of the fight, and, combating with a restless fury, perished amidst a host of enemies.

"I speak briefly, my dear Ferdinando, for these events are too harrowing and terrible to dwell upon. We discovered the accursed traitors, who, won by Bertran de Trevisano's gold, betrayed their mistress. My child's private attendant and a male domestic to whom she was attached, were the miserable wretches who sold body and soul for gold. A powerful narcotic was to have been administered, but by the mercy of Providence, Ellena, without her attendants having perceived it, did not take her usual draught on retiring to rest, consequently she was at once roused from her slumber by the entrance into her chamber of the monster whose vile passions instigated him to murder both mother and child! These miserable tools of the master villain were tried by order of the Council, and put secretly to death by torture.

" Very shortly after this my father died, well stricken in years, to the last bitterly lamenting his inability to take vengeance on the Count of Brescia.

" I must now inform you of a circumstance I was not acquainted with till after my father's death, and this was, that in default of male heirs to the Marchese d'Obizzi, your father, Bertran de Trevisano was the next heir to the Obizzi and Friuli estates, from some deed or compact entered into, I believe, by your great grandfather. I was both astonished and bewildered by this discovery, and consulted eminent lawyers. The important deed with reference to this strange compact is in the iron chest, as well as all other valuable papers.

" Some sixteen months after the loss of your

parents, an event occurred which determined me to leave Venice secretly, and retire and educate you elsewhere. I was accustomed to permit you, with your attendant Mary and two trustworthy domestics, to proceed in our gondola to the little Isle of St. Catherine's, and land and take exercise on the strand. It is quite needless to state full particulars, but the gondola was attempted to be run down by a strange bark, with four men in it, and, but for the timely assistance of two men in a small fishing boat who witnessed, as they supposed, the accident, you would inevitably have been drowned, for the wretches in the strange craft, after upsetting the gondola by striking her in the middle under sail, hoisted additional canvas, and left you and your attendants to your fate. My confidential domestic, Nicholo, who was steering the gondola, vowed it was a premeditated act of the strange craft, for he hailed those on board, and strove all in his power to avoid them, but they purposely altered their course, and steered direct upon the gondola.

" Now, Bertran de Trevisano, though in confinement, might yet have secret agents ; so, by the Count de Merle's advice, I resolved to leave Venice secretly, taking only my attached attendant, Mary, with me.

" Signore Grimani, your father's confidential lawyer, had all the valuable deeds and papers relative to the Obizzi and Friuli estates placed in an iron chest, which was sent to a banker in Florence, and, strange to say, two days after their departure, the office of the Signore Grimani took fire in the night, and was utterly destroyed, with much valuable property in deeds, papers, &c.

"I left Venice, and sailed with you and Mary for Trieste ; there I took the name of d'Alberti and sailed for Naples ; again changed my name to Erizzo ; and finally, after wandering through Italy some months, settled in Spezia and purchased this villa. I then sent for the iron chest and boxes left at the banker's in Florence, and ever since then have kept them under my own eye.

" The miniature of the wretch Bertran de

Trevisano was copied from a portrait in the
Marchese de Trevisano's palace by a young
artist I employed, who was engaged repairing
and cleaning portraits for the Marchese.

"I speak, my beloved grandson, in this very
brief memorial of the past, not of my own
griefs and sufferings.   Since my settling here,
and my acquaintance with Padre Geronimo, I
have learned to bow with more resignation to
the decrees of Divine Providence.   My health
was bad, as you know; day and night I have
been tortured with visions of that terrible
scene—waking or sleeping it haunted my mind
—it preyed upon my heart; I thought of little
else but vengeance; it employed every hour of
my life!   I intended to have imparted all these
particulars to you, my beloved boy, long before,
but, by the advice of Padre Geronimo, I let
them lie in my breast till you obtained more
mature years, and not poison your young life
by instilling into it the venom of revenge.

"Time rolled on; you were placed in the
college in Genoa.   The good Count de Merle,

my best and kindest friend, died. No one knew what became of Bertran de Trevisano when his ten years of imprisonment had expired. After your departure with the Genoese fleet for the Levant, my health rapidly declined; the world was closing up to my view with the memory of the past as strong as ever.

"Oh! my beloved Ferdinando! Leave vengeance to the Lord. Go, seek your rights; take the name and title of your noble race; and oh! my adored Ellena's child, farewell! If I should not live to press you once more to my heart, may the great and just God direct, guide, and protect you.

"ELLENA D'ALBERTI."

Ferdinando d'Obizzi paused; the fading light of the lamp fell upon his pale features; his eyes were filled with tears; for the vision of his mother and his beloved grandmother rose, at it were, before his mind's eye. He bowed his head upon his hands resting on the table, and thus remained during the long hours of the night.

CHAPTER III.

On a clear, lovely day in the early part of
September, a small coasting vessel, impelled by
sail and oar, was running with a steady breeze
past the Lido—bound for Venice—sailing
through the intricate channels, seeking the
entrance of the Grand Canal. On her deck
stood Ferdinando d'Obizzi, his eyes steadily
fixed on the once Queen of the Adriatic,
though she still held her place amidst the
Powers of Europe, not as proudly as two
centuries before, yet with some of her former
glory.

Ten months had elapsed since the death
of Ferdinando's grandmother, the Countess
d'Alberti; time had soothed and softened his
deep grief; forget her virtues, or her love, he
never could. With a naturally buoyant and
cheerful disposition, at two-and-twenty he re-

gained his spirits. His mother's cruel fate, his father's early death, and his vow of vengeance on their murderer, would harass his mind, for he was fully resolved to find Bertran de Trevisano and execute his vow.

After a lengthened conversation with good Padre Geronimo, who tried every argument to induce his young friend to abandon his rash and sinful vow of vengeance, and leave to Providence the punishment of the murderer, he came to the determination of proceeding to Venice, resume his name and rights, and then be guided by circumstances. Against this resolution the Padre had nothing to say, except a wish he expressed to absolve him from his vow. To this Ferdinando objected, for, though a tolerably good Catholic, he doubted the Padre's power.

His grandmother's faithful attendant, Mary, he left with several domestics in the villa, which he retained in his possession, intending it as a quiet retreat from the world; for he was determined not to reside in Venice. His intention was shortly to return, and perhaps take service under the Genoese flag with his friend Durazzo. Taking leave, therefore, of the worthy Geronimo and the faithful and affectionate Mary, he sailed for Livorno. Remaining a few weeks in Florence, he travelled overland to Ravenna— then rapidly ceasing to be a seaport—and embarked, with his chest of deeds, for Venice.

After this short digression, we return to the deck of the " Tartana." It was not without a feeling of great depression that the young Marchese beheld the birthplace of his parents, and his own. The palaces and temples, magnificent as they were, awakened no feeling of pleasure in his heart, for his thoughts were too busy with the past. He could not look upon the " City of the Waters " as his home, for it would continually remind him of the cruel tragedy that deprived him of both parents.

As the " Tartana " came to an anchor, he formed the hasty resolution of disposing of his property in the Venetian Republic, and finding a home in another land.

But Ferdinando d'Obizzi was young, and little acquainted with the ways of the world or society. From the Military College of Genoa he had proceeded to serve for three years in the Levant, with his college friend Durazzo, where he gained considerable renown : his skill with the sword was considered extraordinary, and his great strength and activity unrivalled. But of the world and its allurements, its deceits and its falseness, he knew nothing.

On landing he had his travelling mails and iron chest conveyed to the best hostelry in Venice, the Aquilla Nero. As he passed beneath the splendid arch of the Rialto, he could not but feel admiration at its beauty and the richness of the noble palaces that lined the Grand Canal. Having established himself to his satisfaction in the Aquilla Nero, the following day he procured a gondola, and proceeded to the mansion of the wealthy avocate, the Signore Leone Grimani.

The Palazzo Grimani was situated near the Piazetta of St. Mark. At this time the Signore

Grimani was a widower, his family consisting
of a son and daughter, the former a captain in
the Doge's Body Guard; the latter was in her
nineteenth year.

The Signore Grimani expected the arrival of
the young Marchese, for he had received a
letter from him announcing the death of the
Countess, and of his intention to visit Venice.
The Grimani family once ranked high in
power, and were still remembered with reve-
rence; but, like many other great families, had
fallen victims to State policy and intrigue.
The great great grandfather of Leone Grimani
held the distinguished office of Doge of
Venice, but his descendant, Leone, was obliged
to begin life as an avocate, and be the architect of his own fortune; at the period of
our tale, there were few wealthier men in his
profession in Italy.

Ferdinando d'Obizzi, on being announced
at the mansion of the lawyer, was ushered into
a very handsome saloon, tastefully decorated,
and on the walls hung many valuable paintings

in rather elaborate frames. As the Marchese entered at one door, he caught a glimpse of a female leaving the saloon by another. It was merely a glance, but, brief as it was, he saw a tall and singularly graceful figure. The next moment the Signore Grimani entered the room. He received the young Marchese with great cordiality and much apparent affection of manner, saying—

"You are the image of your parents, whose friendship, I am proud to say, I enjoyed for many years."

Signore Grimani was a good-looking man, about sixty-four or sixty-five years of age.

"Ah!" continued the lawyer, "if the Count de Merle had only lived to embrace the son of his loved and lamented friend"—

"No one," interrupted Ferdinando, "regrets his loss more than myself, Signore Grimani. I have too few friends to lose so good and wise a one without deep sorrow; for, though not personally acquainted with the late Count, all his letters to my lamented grandmother were

read by me, and they always expressed the
kindest and most generous wishes for my
health and welfare; always hoping to see me
before his death."

"But where, my dear young friend—which
I trust you will allow me to call you—where
have you taken up your abode? Surely you
will give me the honour of your company in
my poor mansion till your palace is ready for
your reception."

"My dear sir," returned our hero, "I have
located myself at the Aquilla Nero. Many
thanks for your kind offer. I do not intend
residing in my family mansion. I shall visit
it with a mournful pleasure; but, during my
stay in Venice, I wish to reside at the hostelry
I have selected till I have asserted my rights
and title to the estates of my family."

"There will be no difficulty in doing that,
Marchese," said the lawyer, finding it impossible to induce Ferdinando to change his
mind and take up his abode in his palazzo.
"The fact is, no enquiry of any kind has been

made with respect to the succession of the d'Obizzi property; though I am well aware that with respect to the estates in Friuli and Istria, Bertran de Trevisano is the next heir, supposing you did not exist. Perhaps you are not aware that his brother, the Duke de Malamocco, died a year since, whose title and estates go to the Count de Brescia; for, though twice married, he has left no male heir. Two daughters only survived him; they are handsomely provided for."

" Has any intelligence been received," questioned the Marchese, "of this Count de Brescia, or, as he is now styled, the Duke of Malamocco?"

" No," returned the lawyer, " not publicly. Before the Count de Merle died he mentioned to me a report he had received from some secret agent, that the Duke was thought to be in England, and, it was even said, had married a lady of rank there. But this is, perhaps, after all, only rumour. However, my dear young friend, we shall have time to talk over these matters by-and-by. The first thing to be done is to restore you to your rights and station in society. Let me have the deeds and documents you possess. I wish greatly to peruse the strange deed that makes the Duke of Malamocco your successor in default of male heirs, for I believe, on the other hand, in case of his death, you succeed to some large estate he at present possesses. It all arises, I believe, from some strange will or agreement entered into by your two great grandfathers. Since you will not accept my offer of a suite of rooms in my mansion, I trust you will visit us in a friendly way, that I may have the pleasure of introducing you to my son and daughter."

"Most happy shall I be to make their acquaintance, Signore Grimani," said the Marchese rising, "I will commence this very evening to prove to you how highly I honour and esteem the friend of my parents. I will return to the Aquilla Nero and order my chest of deeds to be brought to your mansion." So saying, after a most cordial leave-taking, the

Marchese retired, much pleased with the Signore
Grimani.

Having seen the chest deposited at the lawyer's, as it was yet early in the day, he hailed a
gondola which was passing ; the gondolier
paused, pushed his boat to the steps, and
touching his cap, said: " Where would the
Signore be pleased to go?"

" Do you know the Palazzo d'Obizzi ? " asked
the Marchese.

" The Palazzo Obizzi !" repeated the man
with a start of surprise. " It is closed, Signore,
these many years. Only one aged couple are
in it."

" I know it is not inhabited," returned the
Marchese. " I merely wish to look at it ; row
me past the front."

The gondolier bowed, plunged his oar into
the water, and, with all the grace and ease of a
Venetian gondolier, urged the light boat into
the Grand Canal.

Passing between the magnificent range of
palaces, the boat glided under the Rialto, and

shortly after the gondolier stopped before the wide front of a noble-looking mansion, whose jalousies were all closed.

"That is the d'Obizzi Palace, Signore; and no other in Venice, at one time, could rival it in magnificence," and the man paused, and then in a low voice added, "and no noble in this great city was higher in rank, or more generous and liberal to those that required his bounty, than the last Marchese d'Obizzi."

Ferdinando was surprised by the man's manner; there was an air of sadness in his tone and look as he spoke; and his gaze the next moment rambled over the deserted mansion so earnestly and so expressively that, as he motioned to him to move on, he felt a very painful sensation at his heart as he himself gazed on the palace where the happiest hours of his parents' lives had passed; and where despair and agony tortured the heart of his mother in her last moments.

The gondolier, apparently in deep thought, listlessly allowed the boat to glide on.

" My good fellow," said Ferdinando, " by
your tone and manner, it strikes me that you
remember the late Marchese d'Obizzi."

" Remember!" repeated the gondolier with
a start, and a flush passing over his intelligent
features, and drawing up his tall figure proudly.
" Signore, I served two years under his command in the Levantine war ; and, more than
that, I can proudly say I was by his side,
cutlass in hand, when he flung himself madly
on the deck of the Turkish Admiral's galley.
Ah ! his was the gallant spirit, Signore,"
solemnly added the man, " in my arms he fell
when he received his death blow, and my arms
bore him back to his own galley." The gondolier passed his hard hand across his eyes, and
then asked in a husky voice : " Where to now,
Signore ? "

For a few moments Ferdinando did not
reply, but at length said—

" Land me at the stairs of the Aquilla Nero."

They soon reached that hotel. Ferdinando,
placing a ducat in the man's hand, said—

" Be with me to-morrow at midday."

The gondolier looked first at the unusual fare he had received and then at our hero, who was leaving the boat.

"Signore, pardon me," he anxiously and almost nervously said, " who am I to enquire for in the hotel? You have paid me like a Prince."

" Enquire for the Signore Erizzo; you will be shown to my room, for I wish to speak to you."

" The Signore Erizzo," said the gondolier in a tone of disappointment, "but I am an old fool," he quickly added, " pardon me, Signore, my memory does sometimes be too busy with the past," and bowing respectfully, he plied his oar, the gondola shot out into the canal and disappeared, slowly gliding from the narrow waters, on whose brink rose the Aquilla Nero, into the broader bosom of the Grand Canal.

CHAPTER IV.

I⊤ is at all times painful to witness deceit and to detect the working of the enemy of mankind in the human breast, corrupting and corroding every impulse, swaying every action, and crushing all the better feelings and energies Nature plants in the human heart.

If it is thus painful to behold the working of the evil spirit in the breast of the young, how doubly sad it is to witness old age a prey to the demon ; and yet how often, with the snows of seventy winters on the brow, with the grave in near perspective, do we see the tottering steps of old age bearing its burden to its last home, while the heart is yet filled with evil thoughts and fierce longings after the empty vanities of this frail world.

Let us enter the mansion of the Signore Grimani, the wealthy lawyer. Let us enter the saloon where the Venetian met Ferdinando d'Obizzi, where he embraced him with all a father's affection, and even shed tears at their meeting. Yet all that was acting, miserable deceit ! For twenty long years this man's life had been a cruel deception. And for what? He had wealth, was respected, had children to cheer his old age, and even his children were reared to gratify his besetting sin. And what was that sin that chilled all the other and better feelings of his heart—made him the hoary-headed hypocrite he was? That foul demon was Pride !

Signore Grimani's great grandfather, Antonio Grimani, died Doge of Venice. That sole thought guided every action of the lawyer's life. His father was a poor mechanic, and his mother a plebeian. When his father died, Leone Grimani was merely a poor clerk to a clever but extremely unprincipled attorney of very low birth, with an only daughter. Leone was a quick, shrewd youth, with his high blood always uppermost in his mind;

his thoughts ever bent upon restoring the lustre of his noble name.

Being a good-looking youth, he succeeded in gaining the heart of the attorney's daughter, whom he married, and was taken into partnership with his father-in-law, who, however, only lived two years after his daughter's marriage, leaving a very handsome fortune to his son-in-law.

Leone Grimani's name and money gave him position, and his business rapidly increased. He counted many nobles as his clients. His children grew up, and he purchased a handsome mansion, furnished it with great taste and elegance, and all went on smoothly till, some few years before the opening of our tale, he became a widower.

In his profession, the Signore Leone Grimani was exceedingly clever, and he gained the esteem of many, and counted as particular friends the Count de Merle and the Marchese d'Obizzi, Ferdinando's father, who entrusted to him the entire control and management

of his large property. The demon Pride
never for a moment quitted Grimani's heart;
his thoughts by day and his dreams by night
were all centred in a desire that his children
should form alliances with noble families; a
difficult task to accomplish in such a city as
Venice, and the more so at that peculiar
period.

The lawyer was, as we have said, wealthy,
but not wealthy enough to tempt the proud
and haughty Venetian nobles to stoop to
an alliance with a lawyer's daughter, whose
father had been a cabinet-maker, and whose
mother was a carpenter's daughter. The
great grandfather was forgotten, and the
Grimani family had cancelled their name
by being concerned in a State conspiracy,
which dispersed and ruined them.

By great efforts and large expenditure,
Leone Grimani got his son Antonio appointed
an officer of the Doge's guard, and, by a
still larger expenditure, raised him, in two
or three years, to the rank of captain.

Every accomplishment that wealth could procure was lavished upon his daughter Bianca, and he gloried in her; and for ten years before the opening of our story had planned an alliance for her.

The reader will pardon this digression, which was absolutely necessary to understand that which is to come.

We return to the saloon, where the Signore Grimani continued pacing backwards and forwards, his hands folded behind his back, his head bent, and his look serious and thoughtful. A side door in the saloon was opened, and his daughter entered. Bianca Grimani was tall and graceful in manner and person, dark eyes, with long silken lashes, and beautifully arched eyebrows. Her luxuriant jet-black hair was braided in front, quite different to the general style of the Venetian dames of rank, who at this period dyed their hair different colours; for her rank, and the time of day, she was rather richly habited, and wore a costly necklace of precious stones round her throat as well as earrings of great value. She was decidedly a hand-some, fine-looking girl, with sparkling eyes, fascinating manners, and a pleasing voice.

"He is gone then, father, and will not take up his abode in our mansion. I wonder why?"

"Why, Bianca, I cannot say," returned the Signore Grimani, looking up, and speaking thoughtfully. "I do not think he will be so easily managed as I expected. He is wonderfully like his mother."

"He is singularly handsome," returned the daughter, with animation in her tone and manner, "and of a stately, noble bearing."

"He is all that," said the old man, thought-fully, and then added in a low voice, "I wonder if he has examined his deeds and papers—I would give much to know."

"You may, I should think, easily ascertain that," said the daughter, seating herself at the table, "by some slight remark in conversation. He does not look—for I could see him well,

and marked the varying expression of his fine
features—but, as I said, I do not think he appears to be a man of business, and most likely
never bestowed a thought on such documents."

"Ha! perhaps not," said the lawyer with
animation, "and if so, I shall have a powerful
lever to work with. I do not think, Bianca,"
he added, looking at his daughter with a
triumphant smile in his face, "I do not think
you will find any difficulty in bestowing your
affections upon the Marchese d'Obizzi.'"

Bianca calmly replied, without any embarrassment of manner—

"None in the least, my dear sir. He would,
if we let him go into Venetian society, capti-
vate the hearts of half the maidens in Venice,
with those dark, beautiful, though somewhat
sad, expressive eyes of his. He has gained a
name by gallant service with our once rivals,
the Genoese, though under the name of Erizzo.
Does he intend taking his own name at once?"

"Certainly. Why not? No one could
dispute his claim to the title and name of the

Marchese d'Obizzi, but his right and title to
the immense estates in Paduan and Istrian territories," added the father in a very low voice,
and bending his head close to his daughter's,
" might not be so easy."

Bianca looked astonished, saying—

" Why, those estates were his father's, were
they not ?   How is that ?"

" Trouble not yourself, my child, with the
why and the wherefore.   If you become
Marchese d'Obizzi, depend on it the estates
will be his."

A servant entered the room, saying that a
great, iron-bound chest had arrived from the
Signore Erizzo, who, having seen it deposited
in the hall, left the key to be delivered to the
Signore Grimani, which key the domestic gave
into the lawyer's hands.

" Let the chest be carried immediately to
my study, and placed in the closet," said the
lawyer, examining the singular-looking key
he held in his hand.

When the servant retired, the Venetian said
to his daughter, holding up the key—

" This shows either great confidence or great carelessness in my young friend, the Marchese d'Obizzi."

Leaving his daughter immersed in thought, the lawyer proceeded to his study, closed the door, locked it, and then opening the closet, gazed anxiously at the chest. As he did so, an exclamation of great joy and triumph escaped his lips, for his eyes rested on the spot where the keyhole ought to be. Over it was a large, flat surface of red wax, and on it was visible the well-known arms of the d'Obizzi family.

Going to the cabinet, he unlocked it, and took from a secret drawer a beautifully engraved seal; he knelt down, and, after a careful examination, said, half-aloud—

" As I expected; a perfect facsimile; they were both executed by the same artist and at the same time. The Marchese kept one, and gave the other to me. Heaven be praised! my task now may be easy; had there been no seal over the keyhole it would have been dangerous to open it; now there is none;" and without a moment's delay, he carefully removed all the wax, though it broke in pieces. These pieces he placed upon the table, and then, inserting the key, opened the chest. It was filled with documents and deeds of all kinds, together with a small casket, which was locked.

Carefully examining every parchment, at length, his eyes sparkling with eager delight, he found three deeds, which he examined one after the other. These three important deeds he locked up in his own iron safe, and replaced them by three old deeds appertaining to the Obizzi family, but of no consequence. He then replaced every document carefully, one by one, in the same order that he found them, and locked the chest.

Lighting a taper, he moulded the pieces of wax and replaced it, melted, over the sliding loops of the keyhole, and then sealed it with the same remarkable seal as before. It was well and cleverly done, and would have defied close scrutiny, though he well knew the young Marchese would tell him to open the chest at his leisure. But the Signore Grimani was re-

solved the seal should not be broken except in
the presence of the Marchese, and not till after
he had ascertained whether the papers had
been examined by himself, thus, in case of
necessity, leaving him the power to replace
those he had changed.

Did not the old man's conscience upbraid
him for this vile deceit towards the son of an
old friend—the orphan child of his benefactor;
for in truth, the patronage of the wealthy
and noble Marchese d'Obizzi was the principal
stepping-stone to his present wealth and position. No; the old man felt no sting of conscience, for the demon Pride was at his elbow
prompting him, whispering—

" Your daughter will be Marchesa d'Obizzi
—your son may aspire to a noble heiress ! "

He arose from his knees with a triumphant
smile upon his lips, and speaking aloud—

" If I could only trace this Count de Brescia
(now Duke of Malamocco), if I could discover
whether he has been married, and whether he
has a son, for I doubt if even he knows that

in default of male heirs, his title and estates go
to this Marchese d'Obizzi and his male heirs.
How strangely that extraordinary and important deed came into my hands!"

For nearly an hour the lawyer kept pacing
the floor of his study; at times murmuring
sentences in a low voice—building schemes of
grandeur and aggrandisement—bestowing not
one thought upon the sixty odd years that had
passed over his head; never dreaming that
already he approached within three or four
of the three-score years and ten—the limit appointed by the Psalmist as the term of man's
existence.

Immediately after the Signore Grimani had
left his daughter in the saloon, a heavy footstep was heard on the stairs, and a pleasant,
musical voice was heard humming gaily a
favourite air. The door of the saloon opened,
and Antonio Grimani entered.

"Ha! my fair sister! all alone; not one
cavalier sighing at your feet, looking as abstracted as—what shall I say, Bianca?—as that
grim old Admiral."

"Or," returned the sister, "as abstracted as my gay brother, Captain Grimani, looks when handing the Doge's daughter into her state barge—will that do, Antonio?"

"Ah!" said the gay Captain, with a forced sigh, "you touch upon a dangerous theme, sister mine. Paulina played me false! but a Marchese's coronet is a pretty, a very pretty plaything; there is no comparison between a captain's plume and that golden circle. I cannot blame her after all."

"Nevertheless, my good brother, take care! People that frequent the Palace say your eyes are always fixed in one direction."

"Curse their impudence and their talk," cried the young man, throwing himself on a sofa, his military equipments making a loud jingle through the saloon.

Antonio Grimani was a handsome young man, some four or five years older than Ferdinando d'Obizzi, though neither so tall nor so powerfully built; he had a fine, showy figure, set off to great advantage by the brilliant uniform of a captain in the Doge's Body

Guard.   A splendid cuirass, richly edged with gold (for he was just off guard), covered his breast ; his doublet quilted and slashed with scarlet satin ; boots as high as half the thigh, but extremely pliant, bending to every movement of the limb ; a richly-worked belt crossing his breast, over the right shoulder, supported his heavy basket-hilted sword, while his heels were ornamented with long, gilt spurs, though in Venice the Doge's Guard never used a horse.

"Tell me, Bianca," demanded her brother, unbuckling his sword and putting it on the table, "tell me what's the news ; for I know by your countenance something unusual has occurred."

"The young Marchese d'Obizzi has arrived in Venice, and has been here," replied Bianca.

" Do you say so ?" returned the Captain with considerable animation, looking his sister keenly in the face.   " I am rejoiced to hear it. What is he like ?   I don't mean as to good looks, for I know he must be a handsome fellow ; all his race were, to judge by the old

portraits in his palace; but as you have seen
him, for I know you have, and you are quick
at reading the human face—is he likely to be
a gay companion? Will he, think you—shall
he and I pull well together?"

"No, Antonio; I do not think you will,"
returned Bianca laughing. "Your dispositions
are not, I will venture to say, at all alike."

"Excellent!" gaily laughed the Captain,
"That's the very reason why we shall become
bosom friends.   Contrast, sister dear; his
purse is a long one and well-filled, and no fear
of a consumption attacking it.   Look at this,"
and Antonio Grimani pulled a handsome em-
broidered purse from his vest and tossed it on
the table, no sound following the action.

"That's a rapid consumption, Antonio," said
Bianca half-seriously, half-laughing, "I filled
that for you out of my private purse only last
night with a hundred ducats!"

"Lost every ducat to that grim old Bambo
this morning, at the Palace.   Lost it in two
throws.   What's a hundred ducats? Bah! as

Monsieur le Baron de Grandbœuf says, when he loses a cool thousand on a throw, and recovers his equanimity with a pinch of snuff sufficient to suffocate a horse."

"One hundred gold ducats in two throws," repeated Bianca, shaking her head seriously, "and to that abominable old gambler, the Admiral; it is really shameful. Where do you think gold is to be found to meet such an infatuation for play as you have imbibed, Antonio? Your father's whole fortune would not stand it. How is it that you never win?"

"Sometimes," replied the brother coolly, "but very rarely. I'll tell you why. Fortune only favours the bold, the timid she despises. My stakes are too small—my purse too lean and hungry. The allowance I get from my father and my pay in the Guards is scarcely enough to pay for my dress and accoutrements. Now, I tell you what, my fair sister," and the Captain looked serious, "I am well aware that my worthy and sagacious sire intends that your fair hand shall be bestowed upon the

handsome Marchese d'Obizzi, who is as wealthy
as Crœsus; for only fancy the sums put by
during his minority—for his worthy grandmother did not spend five thousand ducats a
year out of a revenue of more than a hundred
thousand! By St. Mark! there's a sum!"
and the guardsman paused as if astonished at
the quantity of gold rising in a shining heap
before his mind's eye.

"Well, Antonio," said Bianca, looking
fixedly at her brother, a world of thought resting
on her expressive features, "what does all this,
you are so eloquently holding forth upon,
tend to?"

"A very simple conclusion, sister mine. I
will enlighten you. If all this wealth is to be
thrown at your feet, I, as the only son, and
your most worthy brother, ought surely to be
a participator in it. Now, I will aid you to
bring this most desirable match about, and,
depend on it, you will require my aid."

Captain Grimani, as he looked keenly in his
sister's expressive countenance, perceived a

deep flush come into her cheeks.   He paused
a moment, and then resumed with rather a
satirical laugh.

" You despise my aid, I see.   You fancy
your fascination and beauty will be quite sufficient to take this wealthy noble captive.   Do
not be rash, sister.   The Marchese is only two-
and-twenty.   Do you recollect how I served
you by putting my sword through the body
of the gay French cavalier, the Count St.
Felix?   Ah! the colour on your cheek deepens
and your eyes flash.   You remember this well,
though it is three years ago.   St. Felix was a
splendid fellow for all that."

" Antonio," said Bianca in a tone of repressed
passion, while her eyes flashed as they became
fixed upon her brother, " you know this is a
most painful subject to me ; say what you
want and let this useless recurrence to the past
be dropped.   I was grateful for what you did."

" Well, my fair sister, so you were ; you
were very young, and somewhat giddy ; and
St. Felix, though as handsome a fellow as any

in Venice, was rather volatile, and, what was worse, not rich. There, I will speak no more on the subject. Promise me ten thousand ducats six months after your marriage with the Marchese, and I will do more for you than you imagine."

"There is my hand, Antonio; I agree," said Bianca smiling.

"If I were the Marchese d'Obizzi," said Captain Grimani with his gay laugh, "I would kiss your pretty hand, and I trust before long he will, for fairer in Venice there is none. Now farewell! Depend on it I will make myself particularly agreeable and amiable to this young Crœsus, and before a week expires you will see us bosom friends."

"One word before you go," said Bianca earnestly. "I must request that you never take the Marchese into those vile and fatal saloons of the Ridotto. If he has no passion, and I feel sure he has not, for that hateful vice, do not tempt him."

"You may depend, my dear," returned the

brother, " if I cannot bleed him myself no
other shall."

That evening passed pleasantly and cheer-
fully in the Palazzo Grimani to all. Bianca
was richly and tastefully attired and looked remarkably handsome, and her manner was exceedingly fascinating. She sung and played
on the harp with taste and judgment; and the
young Marchese, who was passionately fond of
music and no bad performer himself, felt
greatly delighted, and, in fact, much struck
with the lawyer's daughter; while Bianca herself was interested, if not captivated, by the
pleasing, easy manners of the Marchese. It
required no acting on her part; susceptible
enough by nature, she required no other
prompting than that of her own heart to en-
deavour to win Ferdinando d'Obizzi's love.
Well accustomed to society, having mixed in
the gay festivities of Venice from a very early
age, she had a great advantage over her intended lover. Skilfully, and with a winning
manner, she induced him to speak of his past

life, of his service in the Levant, of the war, of the beauty of the country, the glories of the Bosphorus, and the various other places visited by the galleys of Genoa. He mentioned the gallant conduct of the young Marchese Durazzo, his early playmate and friend.

"Has your gallant friend, Durazzo," carelessly enquired Bianca, "any brothers or sisters?"

"He has two sisters," returned the Marchese, "but I only saw his sister Julia, his younger sister was educating in a convent. He often spoke of the beauty of his favourite sister Camilla, who was expected home shortly after our return from the Levantine wars."

"It was fortunate for you, Marchese," said Bianca thoughtfully, "that you were not exposed to the danger of looking upon so much beauty, or, perhaps," she added smiling, "you may think it unfortunate."

"If we were unable," was Ferdinando's rejoinder, "to bear even the sight of beauty without falling victims to it, our lot would be a pitiable one. But mere beauty will not win my love, fair lady," added the Marchese, laughing, " if it were worth winning."

" Be not so sure," said Bianca jestingly, " of the adamantine covering you shelter your heart with, Sir Knight. Love's shafts can pierce the finest cuirass of Milan steel."

Thus passed the first evening in the lawyer's mansion.

The Marchese was much pleased with Captain Grimani, who certainly tried to make himself agreeable, and before they parted for the night promised to join in some excursion the Captain planned, in which he contrived that Bianca should be one of the party.

" Will you favour me to-morrow early with a visit," said the Signore Grimani, pressing the hand of the Marchese on parting, " that we may look over those deeds and papers together. I suppose," he added, carelessly, " you have carefully examined them."

" Indeed, my good sir, I have not even looked at them ; but I will attend to your wishes to-morrow ; so good-night," and the Marchese retired to dream of Bianca.

CHAPTER V.

The following day the Marchese d'Obizzi proceeded to Signore Grimani's mansion in the
boat of the gondolier of the previous evening,
whose delight was great in finding in the Signore
Erizzo the son of his old commander.   The
young Marchese made him a handsome present, and engaged his services as long as he
remained in Venice.

The Signore Grimani had passed several
hours of the night in planning projects for the
aggrandizement of his family, through the
means and wealth of the young Marchese
d'Obizzi.   He had other projects in embryo
besides the union of his daughter with the
young man, should, by any chance, that
scheme fail.

When Ferdinando had entered the lawyer's
study, and both were seated, Grimani said—

"My dear young friend, before we proceed
to open yonder chest, I think it better to make
you acquainted with a few particulars of your
family history of which you must be ignorant;
for although your lamented grandmother was
latterly well acquainted with these particulars,
yet she had not, it appears, made you familiar
with them, intending, no doubt, to do so had
not your absence in the Levantine Seas, and
her death, so immediately after your return, pre-
vented her. I will not detain you long, for those
kind of subjects appear dry and tedious to young
men, but, still, they are very important."

"My dear sir," said the Marchese, "I will
listen with great pleasure to anything you have
to say. I am not so averse to business or any
serious subject as my years may lead you to
suppose. Since I became acquainted with the
melancholy history of my ill-starred and
lamented parents my feelings are changed.
I have a purpose to perform, both sacred and
binding, and till that purpose is accomplished
I can call no place or country my home. Any-

thing relative to my family or the past will, therefore, be deeply interesting to me."

As the Marchese spoke, the countenance of the Signore Grimani grew very serious; he nevertheless made no remark, but bowing, proceeded with what he had to say.

"You must know, my dear Marchese, that your grandfather, Nicolo d'Obizzi, and Mare Antonio Trevisano were sworn friends, in fact brothers-in-arms, connected also by distant relationship. They both served with distinguished honour in the armies of the State, and having survived the famous and terrible siege of Famagusta they made a vow, having each saved the other's life in that memorable siege, that if they ever reached Venice they would execute a deed, leaving their great estates each to the other in default of blood descendants male.

"In a miraculous manner they escaped the fate of their commander Bragadino and his garrison. Bragadino, after the surrender of Famagusta to the Turkish Pacha Mustafa, by

honourable capitulation, was ruthlessly seized
by that monster's orders, and, after undergoing
every indignity and torture the wretch could
invent, was finally chained to a staple and slowly
flayed alive. His skin, stuffed with straw, was
then mounted on a cow and paraded through
the streets.* Your grandfather and Mare
Antonio Trevisano attended in his suite when
he surrendered the keys to Mustafa, and were
the only two who escaped being massacred.
They both owed their lives to the ingenuity of
a eunuch, who concealed them, and afterwards
accepted a ransom for their liberty, and after
incredible hardships and escapes, they arrived
safe in Venice.

"Endeared to each other by having passed
through so many perils, on their return they
each executed a deed; your grandfather leaving the whole of his immense estates in Friuli
and Istria, should he die without issue, to the

---

* An historical fact. Bragadino's skin was purchased at an
enormous price by his family and deposited in a sepulchral urn in the
church of S. S. Giovanni, where it remains with a commemorative
inscription.

Count de Brescia and his heirs male, for the estates were strictly entailed; the Count de Brescia executing a similar deed. Both married; your grandfather had two children, a son and a daughter; the latter, however, died in her infancy. Your father inheriting the property, you, as his heir, succeed to it.

" The Count de Brescia died, leaving two sons, the elder lately dead, one of the Council of Ten, though married twice, left no issue male. Bertran Trevisano, the younger son, inherited with the title of Count, the estates in Brescia, of whom little is known—that is, added the Signore Grimani, since his release from imprisonment. It is reported that he was married at the age of thirty-one to some young lady he carried off, but that is mere gossip. In Venice he was considered an unmarried man; but, as I said, from the period of his crime to this time, little is known of him. The Count de Merle insisted upon it that he was in England and married. However, be this as it may, in case of his death without

heir male, you become heir to the immense
estates of the Count de Brescia; and, on the
other hand, should you die without heir male,
all your possessions fall to this Count de
Brescia, or his issue male. Now, I fully expect to find those two important deeds, and
also your grandfather's deeds to the Paduan
and Istrian property, in that chest.

"Many years ago my office—I did not then
live in this mansion—took fire. Fortunately,
a short time before, your father's papers, &c.,
had been removed by the Countess, but I am
not quite satisfied that all his papers were
saved, for they were very numerous, and not
all enclosed in one chest. So you may imagine,
having the interest of your family deeply at
heart, how anxious I am to examine that
chest."

"Well, my dear sir, we will do so at once,"
said the Marchese, whose thoughts at that
moment were elsewhere.

The Signore rose from his seat, and, taking a
knife, removed the seal, and inserting the key,

lifted the lid, the Marchese standing by. As he removed each deed he numbered it, and made a brief entry of its purport on a sheet of paper, till he came to the casket.

"That," said the Marchese, in a tone of sorrow, "contains my poor mother's jewels."

The lawyer placed it on the table and continued his search.

"Very odd," muttered Grimani every now and then, as he folded and put up deed after deed. "Good heavens! How is this," he exclaimed, looking up with an agitated manner and a countenance deadly pale: alas! not from anxiety, but guilt, for that was his first trial of conscience in real crime. His life had been a deception, but not exactly criminal.

"What is the matter, my dear sir?" asked the Marchese earnestly, and with much kindness of manner, "you seem distressed."

The Signore Grimani sat down, having come to the bottom of the chest. He rubbed his head with his handkerchief, and then said—

"I am astounded—alarmed—my dear Mar-

chese; three most important deeds are
wanting. Both the deeds executed by your
grandfather and the Marchese Mare Antonio
Trevisano, and the great title deed to the
estate in the Istrian territory and in Padua are
missing. Could they have been lost by your
grandmother, or destroyed by the fire, years
ago."

"Lost by my dear grandmother! I do not
think it possible; but, as you say, they might,
as they are not in the chest, have been burnt
in the fire; but do not agitate or distress yourself," said the Marchese kindly.

"Not distress myself!" repeated the lawyer.

A loud noise without caused the Signore
Grimani to pause; the next moment the door
was pushed violently open, and a youth of
seventeen or eighteen years of age burst into
the room, singing and whistling and clapping
his hands by turns.

"Ha! ha! ha! uncle, here I am in spite
of them. Ho! ho! how funny—who's he?"
pointing with his finger at the astonished

Marchese d'Obizzi ; while, with the perspiration pouring from his head, and a terrible expression on his features, the Signore Grimani recovered himself and started from his chair.

" Ha ! ha ! uncle, don't touch me. I won't tell ; saw you yesterday : I peeped through the hole : I saw you break the seal and open—"

By this time Signore Grimani had contrived to seize the unfortunate imbecile by the collar and drag him from the room, just as two domestics came hurrying to his assistance.

The Marchese remained alone in the room astonished at the scene. He was not so much surprised at the strange appearance of the poor youth, who he at once discovered was weak in intellect, though there was nothing repulsive either in his face or person. In figure he was extremely slight, but well formed ; his face thin, and very pale, but the features, when not distorted by the violent gestures, were good ; his hair was closely cropped, and his garments neat and well-conditioned. But what surprised our hero was the change that came

over the features of the lawyer when he beheld
the boy and heard his words, which the Marchese did not at all understand.

In a few minutes the Signore Grimani returned; his features restored to their natural
repose, though his manner when he spoke was
evidently agitated.

" You must think this all very strange, my
dear young friend," said the lawyer, sitting
down, " and unaccountable ; but the fact is, we
all feel more or less, and yet ought not, the
exposure of family infirmity ; that poor lad
you saw is the orphan of a distant relative, and
left totally destitute by the loss of both parents,
and born, as you beheld him, with weak intellect. I took pity on the unfortunate child
and brought him up, keeping him generally
confined to a suite of rooms in the back of the
mansion, and letting him out at times, when
least under the influence of his terrible malady,
for at times he is quite ungovernable. How
he got out now I know not, for he has a steady,
elderly dame to take care of him. Indeed, he

was to have gone yesterday to—" the Signore Grimani slightly hesitated and then continued —"to a relation at Fusina, where he will have the benefit of a change of air and a large garden to take exercise in. Poor boy! Bianca is so kind-hearted that she insisted on keeping him in the house. She often plays her lute to him, for music has a wonderful effect, making him quite rational for the time; but I again entreat pardon for allowing this incident to disturb us from matters so important."

"Make no apology for an action that only shows kindness of heart, and your fair daughter's gentleness and sweetness of disposition."

The Signore Grimani bowed, sighed, and then said—

"You are very good, Marchese, to look upon this affair so kindly. We will now, if you please, resume — where were we interrupted—I think you were requesting me not to distress myself at the singular loss (I trust

not, though I say it) of those three deeds and
papers. But the consequences may be terrible,
though, as yet, no enquiry has been set on foot
by any of the persons concerned. What I
mean by persons concerned is this: Those
great estates you succeed to were purchased
by your grandfather from the noble family of
Contarini. Should the present members of
that family question the legality of that purchase—say that the term of years had expired
—we have no means whatever to establish
your claims ; or, again, should the Count de
Brescia die without issue male, your title to
the estates would be disputed by the next
heirs."

"And very justly, my dear sir," returned the
Marchese very calmly. "You must confess it
would be a very hard case to be deprived of
the property of one's ancestors by the caprice
or romantic vow of two enthusiastic friends.
The Brescian estates ought in justice to de-
scend to the next of kin by blood ; and, having
enough of my own, I should feel very loth

to deprive the rightful heirs of their property."

The Signore Grimani let his gaze rest on the
floor for a moment, and then, looking up,
and smiling, said—

"You are young and kind, and noble-
hearted ; but you look upon this act of your
grandfather in a wrong light ; however, as this
is a remote contingency, we will not talk of it.
I will speak on a more probable event. Should,
by any extraordinary accident, or, by strange
or unaccountable event, the circumstances of
these deeds being lost, come to the ear of the
Contarini family, they might make claims that
would involve years of litigation ; and, perhaps,
in the end, deprive you of your just rights.
Understand me, this is only a supposition. I
am a man bred and born in the quibbles of the
law, and look upon those things in a different
light than you do."

"My kind friend," said the Marchese rising,
and, with a cheerful smile, laying his hand
upon the old man's shoulder, "do not let us

torment ourselves with plunging into the future, and lamenting an event that may never take place. Those papers or deeds appear to be lost, and yet they may not be; but this I assure you, if they are, and the estates go after them, the event will neither break my heart nor affect my spirits. I was never accustomed to luxuries; my youth has been passed in a rough field. I have one purpose to perform, and if I am stripped of those two great estates you speak of, I have still enough left for all my wants and my purpose. Now let us drop the subject, for I have promised your fair daughter to accompany her to San Giorgio Maggiore, and it is now the appointed time."

"Be it so," returned the lawyer, pressing the Marchese's hand with a pleased and gratified smile; "Bianca would never forgive me if she knew I plunged you into the labyrinths of the law, instead of letting you be entangled in the weaker meshes of a lady's net."

"Do not say weaker, my good sir," replied the Marchese, laughing—"a worse labyrinth,

I fancy, to disentangle one's self from than all your wilderness of law technicalities."

So saying, he left the lawyer in his studio, and proceeded to the saloon, where he found the Signora Bianca turning over some music.

She looked up with a very fascinating smile as Ferdinando d'Obizzi entered, and held out her hand, which, being a very fair, small hand, the Marchese carried to his lips according to the gallantry and custom of the period. But perhaps the kiss was more than mere gallantry required, for a slight flush passed over the lady's cheek as her eyes met those of the Marchese. As he led her to a seat, she said—

"I was afraid my worthy father, once mounted on his hobby, which the law is, would keep you till your patience would be exhausted —and, by-the-by, you were interrupted by my poor weak-headed cousin—poor fellow!" and her voice fell and she spoke feelingly. "I cannot bear to send him amongst strangers. I assure you he is quite harmless, nay, at times, even rational. I play to him occasionally for hours."

"You are very good and very kind to do so," said the Marchese. "Poor youth! It is not only a sad misfortune to him, but a sadder to those who have to administer to his wants."

The fair Bianca gave a gentle sigh, and then, changing the conversation, they set out to join the party to San Giorgio Maggiore, where three or four hours were pleasantly spent. The evening was passed in singing, music, &c. Bianca's chance of a splendid matrimonial alliance was progressing favourably, for the young Marchese's thoughts had taken a widely different scope since his arrival in Venice.

CHAPTER VI.

IT soon became known in Venice that the Marchese d'Obizzi had returned to claim the title, estates, and possessions of his ancestors. This intelligence did not create much surprise amongst the higher orders, for it was pretty well known that he had been educated in some continental city from his boyhood; his grandmother having taken a violent aversion to Venice.

There were, however, several distant relations and connections of the Obizzi family who rejoiced in the return of the young Marchese, whose possessions, increased by a long minority, were known to be princely. These persons made a point of calling to welcome the young heir, for they fully expected the Obizzi Palace would be reopened with princely splendour. The personal appearance of the young man created quite a sensation, especially amongst the fair aspirants for a high matrimonial alliance.

But when a fortnight had passed and no sign of preparation going on in the Obizzi Palace, which remained closed as usual, and its master continued to reside at the hotel, the Aquilla Nero, and visited only the mansion of the Signore Grimani, remarks, inuendoes, surmises, &c., &c., were freely uttered in confidence one to the other.

The Marchese was seen constantly with the gay Captain Grimani and a great friend of his, a certain French cavalier, who gave himself the name of Baron Henri de Chateaunœuf; who lived in a very good style at a first-rate hotel; and who was known to be a constant frequenter of the Ridotto Saloons, and accounted a remarkable favourite of the Goddess Fortune, and also a very formidable opponent with a weapon —then very much in use—the small sword.

Captain Grimani had introduced the Baron de Chateaunœuf to our hero, and this gentleman, with a good exterior, plausible manners, and easy appearance, performed his part well—it was but performing—not having the most remote right to either the title or name of Chateaunœuf. Tall and vigorous in person, in age not more than six or seven-and-twenty, dark complexion, good eyes, and coal-black hair and moustachios, he was a very fair specimen of a French Baron of that period, and yet, though full of conversation and anecdote, and apparently well acquainted with several European Courts, and most assiduous in his attentions to Ferdinando Obizzi, our hero neither liked nor admired him.

The Doge of Venice at this time was Carlo Contarini, destined to wear the Ducal Coronet for a very brief space indeed; scarcely thirteen months. His son, Marco Contarini, was one of the most ambitious youths in the Republic. Besides being ambitious and proud of his high descent (which scorned to mix with plebeian blood to rebuild the somewhat ruined fortunes of his proud family), he was crafty, mean, and singularly avaricious for one so young, for he was only four-and-twenty. His two sisters were remarkably handsome. His father ascended the Ducal Throne a few months before the Marchese d'Obizzi's visit to Venice, at a time when the Venetians obtained some splendid victories over the Turks. Great rejoicings accordingly took place. The Venetians, a fête-loving people, thought of nothing but balls, masquerades, mock tournaments, sham naval fights, and regattas of all sorts. At this period the Republic was sinking gloriously.

To Ferdinando d'Obizzi's rights and claims there was no kind of opposition ; he was received everywhere with smiles and welcomes. The Doge honoured him with an interview and a general invitation to the Ducal Palace. The young Marchese had reason to be satisfied, and, as far as his reception in society went, he was so. But he was not quite satisfied with himself. He was, he fancied, in love with Bianca—and yet he was not in love—his love was a contradiction ; in her presence he was fascinated; latterly, when he returned to the Aquilla Nero, he became thoughtful and abstracted, he dreamed less of Bianca, but *thought more.* How was this? Was the maiden less beautiful, was her manner less kind, less fascinating? No, his conscience answered;—had he seen any one he admired more? No, was still the answer. However, if Ferdinando d'Obizzi was not quite certain whether he was in love or not, the lady was quite the reverse, for her whole heart and soul were devoted to the young Marchese.

One morning, after about two months' residence in Venice, Ferdinando d'Obizzi took his way as usual to the Mansion of Signore Grimani. After spending nearly an hour on business with the lawyer relative to the accumulated revenues, as well as to their disposal, he ascended to the saloon. Signora Bianca was not there; but, instead, he encountered the Baron de Chateaunœuf coming out.

After saluting the Marchese, the Baron said—

"I am going to Captain Grimani's Salón des Armes—will you join us? We usually have a little practice once a week; is is useful to keep the hand in."

"I have no objection," said the Marchese, turning round and following the Baron, who led the way along the gallery into a remote wing of the mansion; and, opening a door, they entered a very large chamber entirely devoted to the practice of arms. There was no furniture, if we except a table and a few chairs, but the walls were tastefully decorated with various weapons, hung fancifully, consisting of swords, pistols, arquebusses, fowling-pieces, &c., neither very light nor very scientific in their construction, but richly mounted, together with foils and masks in abundance.

"Ah! Marchese, I am rejoiced to see you here," said Captain Grimani, who was just then selecting a foil. "The Baron and I take a turn at this kind of amusement now and then. I am only a very mediocre performer. Our friend here is perfect."

" Mon Dieu! No," interrupted the Baron. " In Paris every tenth cavalier you met would be my master. My countrymen are extravagantly fond of the small sword. Do you like the exercise, Marchese ? "

" I was passionately fond of it once," returned our hero, while the Baron stripped off his coat, and selected a mask and foil.

" Well, you and I, Marchese," said the Captain, " will have a trial, after I get a lesson from the Baron," and, putting on his mask, the young man commenced.

In less than a minute, the Marchese, who was, perhaps, scarcely to be surpassed in the use of the foil and the small sword, perceived that the Captain was no match for the Baron, and in five minutes more, that the Frenchman was no match for himself.

After several very palpable hits, the Captain gave in, saying—

" I have no chance with you, Baron ; none whatever."

" Still," returned the Frenchman, with no

small degree of conceit in his manner, "you are improving."

"What chance should I have with you, Marchese," said Grimani, wiping his forehead and adjusting his mask, while the Baron offered a foil and mask to the Marchese.

"Well," returned Ferdinando, laughing and taking the foil, "you were not in earnest with Monsieur le Baron, were you?"

Had the Marchese looked round at the Frenchman, he would have been somewhat astonished at the singular expression that passed over his features.

"The deuce! do you say so," said the Captain, "then I give you up to the Baron at once. I like to see two skilful fencers."

There was a slight hesitation in the Baron's manner, but whatever caused it, he recovered his usual bearing in a moment, laid aside his mask, as he perceived the Marchese had done, and laughing, said—

"You are easily daunted, Captain."

The Marchese d'Obizzi did not take off his

doublet, but very quietly took his place opposite his antagonist. Their foils crossed, the next minute the Baron saw his strike against the ceiling. A smothered oath escaped his lips; the next moment he laughed heartily, saying—

"We must acknowledge you our master. I bow, Marchese, to your superior skill."

"Then I say you are easily daunted, Monsieur le Baron; for after all that is but a trifle, and easily learnt."

"Yes," returned the Frenchman, picking up his foil, "but to perform it requires a very powerful wrist and great skill. Let us try without that feat."

No better luck attended the Baron; his passes were all foiled, and every time the Marchese pleased he buttoned him, till, in a fit of anger and disgust, he threw the foil from him.

"Ha! my dear friend," said Captain Grimani, laughing, though a keen observer might easily have detected that his manner was constrained, "your pre-eminence in the small sword is over. I must take lessons from another master. Are you as good a shot with the pistol, Marchese, as you are matchless with the foil, for, I assure you, our friend the Baron has hitherto stood unrivalled."

"Well, we can try our skill with the pistol," said the Marchese, who had his own reasons for showing his skill, for no particle of vanity was there in the display of his superiority.

Whether the Baron concealed his skill or not with the pistol, we cannot say, but the Marchese beat his antagonist two out of every three shots.

Shortly after this they gave up the amusement, and returned to the saloon, where they found the Signora Bianca and an elderly lady, a distant relation, who generally accompanied her in her excursions when attended by the Marchese d'Obizzi. The conversation turned upon the great public masquerade that was about to be given at the Ducal Palace in honour of the recent victories over the Turks. Several saloons were to be thrown open to the public under certain regulations, while the entrée to the Duke's private saloons was restricted to those holding personal invitations and tickets. The Marchese had received one from the Palace that morning. None but the high nobles were honoured with these invitations.

"You will go, of course," remarked Bianca to the Marchese. "In what character do you intend appearing?"

"Indeed, fair lady, I am not inclined to support any other character than my own, and shall content myself simply with a domino; in fact I feel no very great inclination for masquerades in any shape. All maskers, I understand, are required to remove their masks on entering the saloons set apart for the Doge and his guests. A very good and proper arrangement."

"Which puts an end," remarked the Baron, with a sneer, "to all the mystery and intrigue so fascinating to all Venetians."

"By Saint Mark!" said the Captain, "I

shall be well content to pass the evening with
the mass in the lower saloons; depend upon
it, Bianca, there is where the mirth will be
'fast and furious,' and you must come too,
Marchese, or else Bianca will say you despise
our untitled race."

"There you wrong me, brother," returned
Bianca quietly, just as Ferdinando was about to
reply, "I think I know the Marchese's thoughts
better than you, with all your acuteness, and
that no evil idea has a place in his mind, for,
be it known to you, he has promised to be
protector to myself and our friend here, the
Signora Pisani, at this gay fête."

The Baron looked at Bianca with a peculiar
expression of countenance, but she turned
away her head, saying to the Signora Pisani,
a lady descended from a good family—

"Now, my dear friend, I depend on you as
to selecting a dress."

"Pray take that of a Novice," said the
Baron, in rather a marked tone.

"Come, come," said the Captain, "let them

keep their choice of dress to themselves, it will be an amusement finding them out. What do you say, Marchese, to a stroll on the Piazetta?"

"Not now," said our hero, "I may, perhaps, join you there in an hour. I have to meet a person at my own mansion respecting some repairs;" and, after a few words with the Signora Bianca, the Marchese left the dwelling of the lawyer.

After spending an hour, pointing out to an architect of eminence some repairs and additions which he wished done to the Palace d'Obizzi, which he daily visited, finding a melancholy pleasure in strolling through the noble saloons where his unfortunate parents had passed so many happy hours, he returned to his hotel.

As yet the Marchese had done without any personal attendants; of simple habits, and having but few wants, and by no means settled as to his future proceedings, he contented himself with the attendance of the domestics of the hotel; his name and rank being now known, the best suite of rooms had been allotted him.

On entering his sitting-room, one of the servants presented him with a letter, saying—

" It was left here, my lord, by a stranger to us."

Ferdinando d'Obizzi took the letter carelessly, and when the man had retired, looked at the direction. He knew nothing of the handwriting, which appeared to be that of a female; the direction was simply " The Marchese d'Obizzi."

"Who can this be from?" thought our hero, breaking the seal. "I have no correspondent in Venice of the softer sex."

The first words interested him ; it ran thus—

" Ferdinando d'Obizzi. This warning comes from one who once dearly loved your beautiful mother. Pay attention to it, for it may save you from after regret and perhaps intense suffering. Take heed then, how you permit the fascination of the senses to lead you to imagine that your heart is touched. Marchese d'Obizzi, you have not yet seen the being that ought to win the love of the child of Ellena, neither do I believe you know your own heart. But be warned; at the Masque at the Ducal Palace wear a blue and silver domino—you shall learn more; but till then, beware of the false Baron de Chateaunœuf, and believe one, though unknown,

" YOUR SINCERE FRIEND."

The writing was in the hand of a female, and a remarkable handwriting it was. It was plain to him, therefore, as he finished the perusal of the billet, that his motions and actions were carefully noted, and by one to whom his mother was known. The purport of the letter was evidently to warn him against placing his affections upon the lawyer's daughter, and against companionship with the French Baron. He was himself convinced, false or not, that the Baron was an unfit companion for him; moreover, he disliked him. Little as he was

acquainted with society, he was naturally of
too high a spirit and too refined a mind to
feel any predilection for the amusements and
pursuits of Captain Grimani and his friend the
French Baron.   The latter, let his imitation
be ever so good, he felt certain was no gentleman in manners or conversation.   Still he was
received by some of the first families in Venice
where play was countenanced, and where he
kept a strict guard upon his words and actions.
The Marchese, in the commencement of their
acquaintance, did not suspect his false rank;
he never was intimate with him ; but latterly
he began to detect certain strange words and
doubtful actions in Captain Grimani's friend,
and from that moment dropped all intercourse
with him, except when meeting him at Signore
Grimani's.   Therefore the warning against the
French Baron he was disposed to take in the
friendly light it was given in the letter of the
unknown.

With respect to the hints thrown out against
his apparent attachment to the Signora Bianca,

he felt uneasy and unhappy. In love he certainly was not—he now felt firmly convinced of that; but was he convinced that his attentions and fondness for the lady's society had not induced love on her part. If so, could he in honour recede? It is true he had never spoken of love to Bianca; besides, his heart smote him for ever thinking of love. Had he forgotten his vow—" Never to form any tie of happiness while the murderer of his mother lived."

Ferdinando d'Obizzi reproached himself severely for his want of decision and weakness in permitting himself to be fascinated or pleased when he had a sacred duty to perform. At one moment he came to the resolution of leaving Venice at once and travelling, when he might, perhaps, come upon some trace of the Duke of Malamocco. But he could not leave Venice until after the Masked Ball at the Ducal Palace. He also determined to have an interview with the Signora Bianca Grimani, for in his heart he was the soul of honour.

Somewhat unsettled of purpose, and naturally of a disposition to feel and enjoy the fascination of female society, in his interview with Bianca he would candidly state how he was situated—his vow, and his determination of abiding by it. If in this interview she reproached him with having, by his attentions and apparent fondness for her society, won her love, he would then become a suitor for her hand, on the sole condition of his fulfilling his vow previously.

As the Marchese came to the latter determination, he felt a strange feeling or presentiment of evil creeping over him.

"I have acted unwisely," he muttered, as he roused himself from his thoughts and reflections; "I do not love as I ought to love, and yet I am going to plunge into an engagement that will fetter me for life."

Disappointed with himself and his conduct, the young Marchese passed an uncomfortable evening. He did not visit the lawyer's mansion that night; neither did he join the Captain

Grimani and his constant companion the
French Baron in their evening amusements.
He did not even stir abroad, but remained
writing a long letter to the kind friend and preceptor of his childhood, Padre Geronimo, to
whom he laid bare his heart, and requested his
advice for the future guidance of his conduct ;
lamenting extremely his having remained so
long in a city that in reality he felt but little
interest for, and which constantly reminded him
of the misfortunes of his parents.

CHAPTER VII.

THE morning before the fête at the Ducal Palace, Ferdinando d'Obizzi received a letter from Signore Grimani, requesting to see him immediately, excusing himself for not being able to visit him in person, feeling very unwell.

The Marchese, wondering what could occasion so sudden a summons, set out in his gondola for the Grimani Mansion. On being shown into the lawyer's study, he found the old man looking very pale and considerably agitated.

" You must excuse me, my dear Marchese," said the lawyer, " in taking the liberty of sending for you, but I assure you what I have to speak about is of great importance, and has caused me, connected as I have been for years with your family, much unhappiness."

"I am very sorry to see you so distressed, my good sir, and beg you will not agitate yourself on any subject that has reference to my affairs, in the manner you do."

"You are very kind, my dear young friend," returned the Signore Grimani, with a sad smile, and pressing the Marchese's hand, "but this promises to be too serious an affair to consider lightly," and, taking up a folded paper, he opened it, and, handing it to the Marchese, begged him to peruse it.

The letter was directed to the Signore Grimani, and was as follows:—

"My respected Friend,—

"You will greatly oblige me by letting me know when it will be convenient to you to permit me to cast my eye over the Deed of Purchase and the Title Deeds of the Estates in Padua and Istria now held by the young Marchese d'Obizzi. His Highness, the Doge, in looking over some old documents belonging to his family, found one relative to the estates in question, which, you know, were originally purchased from the Contarini family. This document, it seems, throws a doubt upon the validity of the purchase, &c., &c.

"Doubtless this is mere surmise ; but, as I am his Highness's lawyer, I cannot refuse his request to look at the title deeds, which, I feel perfectly satisfied, are quite legal and correct. Half-an-hour will set the question at rest for ever, for, singularly enough, those deeds have no duplicates or copies, and no one has seen them for years. Excuse the trouble I am giving you.

"Your faithful friend,

LUIGI MALAPERT.

"Venice, Oct. 16th."

Having read the letter carefully and returned it to the Signore Grimani, the Marchese said—

"All that is very singular, coming now after a lapse of nearly a century since that purchase was made by my grandfather from Leonardo Contarini. I understand little of the law, but, I suppose, having lost those deeds, I lose the estates, as the witnesses are so long since dead."

"Heaven forbid!" said the lawyer, "that such should be the case. The deeds are missing, certainly. I have spent days in searching lumber-rooms where many papers and deeds were thrown after the fire that consumed my office, but unsuccessfully. I doubt much what my learned brother of the law says about finding such a document as he speaks of; that is, I think, a ruse. It is well known that many valuable papers were burned in my office, and it was also known that I had in my possession all your father's deeds and papers. At that time our present Doge held a high command in the East, and remained there many years. By a singular chance your grandmother removed all the most valuable documents of your family from my care only a day or two before the fire, or, unquestionably, they would have been consumed."

"What do you purpose doing?" demanded

the Marchese, " in this case, not having any
deeds to show."

"We must meet ruse with ruse, my dear
young friend. I will request to see the document my brother lawyer speaks of, and
finally refuse to show the deeds, denying his
right to peruse them."

"That will lead to a tedious litigation, will
it not?" demanded d'Obizzi.

" It will gain time, Marchese; time is everything. We are aware that your claims are
undeniable, and, though these deeds are missing, your cause is a righteous one, and it is
your duty to defend the property left to you
by your noble and lamented father. Recollect,
my dear young friend, if defeated in this case
you would not only lose the estates, but be
stripped of everything you possess to make
up the vast sums received ever since the
original purchase of the property."

The Signore Grimani looked fixedly in the
young man's face, but all there was calm and

collected, a quiet smile playing over his hand-some features as he said—

"There are three things, my dear sir, of which they can never deprive me, and whilst I hold them my spirit and my heart will be un-subdued. My honour, this right arm," holding out one of great strength, "and this trusty friend," and he touched his plain, unadorned good steel that hung by his side, " will defend my right.   To defend that right, my dear sir, I am both willing and ready ; but if, through misfortune or injustice I lose that right, be it so.   It shall not cost me a sigh."

The Signore Grimani's features underwent a singular change, but he hid them from his young friend by passing his hand across his brow; he uttered not a word for a minute, and then, rising, said—

"We must not anticipate evil, my dear Marchese.   I am not very well to-day, but, depend on it, your interests shall be attended to.   I do not give up all hope of those deeds yet. You will find Bianca alone. I will answer this letter cautiously."

Ferdinando d'Obizzi, in a thoughtful mood, ascended the stairs to the family sitting-room, and found Bianca seated at a table, leaning her head on her hand, an open book before her, and her features bearing rather a troubled expression. She started up from her musing position as soon as she heard the Marchese's step, and, with a pleased smile, held out her hand, saying—

"I thought, Marchese, you had become tired of us. Where were you last evening? We wondered at your absence."

Bianca looked positively beautiful; there was less colour in her cheek, but there was a sparkling brightness in her eyes, and a softness in the whole expression of her features that became her well. She was less richly dressed than usual, but with great taste. She had keenly observed all Ferdinando's predilections; plain and unostentatious himself, though singularly elegant and simple in his dress, he greatly disliked the heap of finery, and the great display of jewels, and satins and velvets, in which the Venetian dames indulged on every occasion.

Bianca had observed this, and, though naturally fond of excess of jewels and dress, abandoned them immediately she discovered Ferdinando's taste. Bianca's real feelings and disposition will be developed in our story.

"Since my arrival in Venice," said the Marchese, seating himself by Bianca's side, "now nearly twelve or fourteen weeks, last evening was the only one in which I have deprived myself of the pleasure of your society."

"That sounds very well, Sir Knight," said Bianca, with a pleasant smile ; "but what kept you away, as you say it was a deprivation?"

" In truth, depression of spirits to a certain degree, and a wish to write a long letter to the kind preceptor of my youth, Padre Geronimo. But, fair Bianca, will you spare me half-an-hour of your time to speak to you on a somewhat serious subject?"

The colour in Bianca's cheek vied with the colour of the rose, and she felt herself tremble all over—Bianca was, in truth, in love!

Just as Ferdinando was about to speak, and lay before the maiden a recital of his early years, his vow, and his determination how to proceed in his future career, a heavy footstep was heard, the door opened, and the Baron de Chateaunœuf entered the room. A disagreeable smile crossed his features as he saluted the Signora Grimani and held out his hand to the Marchese, saying to Bianca—

" I expected to find your brother; he is not on duty to-day; he promised to meet me here, that we might go and order our intending costume for to-night."

The curl of Bianca's lip, and the tone of her voice, betrayed the dislike she felt to the presence of the French Baron. She, however, replied—

" You must seek my brother elsewhere, for

you are late; he left the house ten minutes since, and when once he goes out is not very likely to return."

The Baron showed no symptom of moving, and the Marchese, after joining in some unmeaning conversation, commenced by the Frenchman, took up his plumed beaver, and telling Bianca he would be sure to be punctual in the evening, with a meaning look, left the saloon, whilst Bianca, with a cold salutation to the French Baron, quitted the room by another door.

The Frenchman very coolly humming a well-known French air, ending with the words *Je suis de trop*, followed the Marchese downstairs. The latter heard the words, and understood the Frenchman's meaning; and stopping under the great portal, laid his hand quietly on the Baron's shoulder, saying, in a calm voice—

" The next time, Baron, you meet me in a lady's presence, please to select other words than those you have just used so rudely. I perfectly understand your meaning."

"You are using strange words, Marchese d'Obizzi," said the Frenchman, colouring violently, his dark brow fiercely contracting as he bent his eyes upon the undisturbed features of the Marchese.

"If you do not like them, Monsieur le Baron de Chateaunœuf," and he pronounced the last word with so marked an emphasis, and so unmistakable a smile, that the Baron's colour changed from red to white, "you have your remedy, and that is, keep out of the way of hearing them for the future."

The Frenchman stood rooted to the spot, whilst our hero slowly passed on, and entered his gondola. For several minutes the Baron remained gazing at the receding boat. He clenched his hand firmly, and shook it in the direction of the departing gondola, and a withering curse came from between his lips. As the sound died away, a hand was laid upon his arm, and a voice whispered in his ear—

"He smells a rat, Monsieur le Baron de Chateaunœuf."

Turning slowly round, not showing any surprise at the words of the speaker, the Baron said —

" His sense of smelling, Jaques, may cost that proud boy very dear."

The person who had addressed the Baron was a man of middle height, about thirty years of age, with a cunning cast of countenance, a good figure, and somewhat gentlemanly appearance. He was also a Frenchman, and held the situation of valet to Captain Grimani.

" Where is your master, Jaques ? And how came you to be so keen an observer of this young Marchese ?"

" Ha! ha! ha!" laughed the valet, " you forget that I am acting a part, Monsieur le Baron, as well as yourself. We have both our cards to play, though differently. Just move on towards the canal; I see one of the domestics coming this way. We can enter a gondola, for my worthy master told me to watch for you, and to bring you to him."

The valet, Jaques Maletot, hailed a gondola, and both entered beneath its awning.

"Land us at the Piazetta," said the Baron, and the gondola was urged on its way.

"You thrust yourself in, Monsieur le Baron," said the valet, " at a very malapropos moment this morning; the young gentleman was actually popping the question. I was listening at a side door. I don't like this, 'tis a bad omen. What will the Captain say?"

"Curse the Captain!" returned the Baron. "We are duped; that is, you and I are, for the Captain is not in our part of the plot."

"*Sacre Diable!* How so?" questioned the valet.

"Why, curse the girl, she's in love— desperately in love with the Marchese."

A half-smothered whistle came from the lips of Jaques Maletot, on hearing this communication.

"That alters the case wonderfully. Then she will sell you, Monsieur le Baron, and hold fast by the Marchese. *Sacre !* She is playing a bold game after that affair with the Count St. Felix. Depend on it, if the Marchese hears a whisper of that matter, she has as much chance of being Marchesa d'Obizzi as your worship of being Baron de Chateaunœuf," and the valet laughed. "You are silent, Baron," continued Jaques Maletot. "I am afraid you are in love with the girl yourself."

The Baron looked fiercely at the valet, who only laughed, as, putting his head outside the awning, he said—

"Here we are."

The next moment they landed. The Baron walked across the quay, followed by Jaques, and taking his way through several of the narrow streets, or rather causeways, at the back of the palace, entered the open door of a large, uninviting-looking mansion, the valet following at a little distance. After ascending a flight of dirty steps, a door barred their further progress; two peculiar knocks, and the door swung back of its own accord, and they passed

in and found themselves in a long gallery, but
no sign of inhabitants. There were several
doors; stopping at one, the same kind of
knock was repeated, a heavy bolt was drawn
back by a spring, and the door opening, the
Baron and Jaques Maletot entered the room.
It was a large, well-furnished chamber, lighted
from a skylight, having no other windows. At
a table, on which stood several flasks of wine
and some handsome Venetian glasses, sat
Captain Grimani. On a side table were
numerous masquerade dresses and masks. This
saloon, and one or two others, composed what
was then designated the " Casino " of the gay
Captain Antonio Grimani, a man of the most
corrupt and depraved morals in the renowned
city of Venice. Most of the nobility and
wealthy citizens hired mansions at the back of
the Piazetta, which they called their " Casinos."
Captain Grimani, if not one of the wealthiest
of Cavaliers, was certainly one of the most
extravagant and licentious. His liberal allowance, and his pay as a Captain in the Doge's

Body Guard, were quite inadequate to support his extravagance, let alone his inconsiderate thirst for play; and, besides these vices, he drank hard, and was fond of low company, and as none of these choice amusements could be enjoyed in his father's mansion, the gay Captain hired a " Casino," where he could not only enjoy himself to his heart's content, but where he also kept company with very dangerous associates.

To return to the Baron, who on entering the room threw himself on a chair, as did also Jaques Maletot, not at all heeding the presence of his worthy master; nor did the Captain evince the slightest surprise.

" You look moody, *amico*," said the Captain, filling his glass, and examining a piece of paper very much resembling a bill or order of the present day. " Has anything new happened this morning?"

" Nothing very pleasant," returned the Baron, while Jaques Maletot, after helping himself to a glass of sparkling wine, took up

the paper the Captain had been looking at, and
began a strict investigation of its contents.
"In the first place, our coffers are empty;
secondly, the young Contarini, who is as greedy
of gold as a miser of four-score years and ten,
demands payment of that cursed, ill-judged
bet of yours, that you would score thirty in
three throws, and the dice you had in your
pocket at the time, true ones."

"Yes, yes, you may grumble now, Baron,"
growled the Captain, savagely. "Whose fault
was it that they were true dice, eh? You said
in the morning, when I went out, that you had
changed them. I did not think at the time
what you meant, for my head ached con-
foundedly after the night's debauch, so when
Contarini laughed at my saying I could throw
so and so, I offered to bet him a thousand
sequins I would score thirty in three throws.
He instantly took my offer, and curse it, I
threw only eighteen, and not only lost my
money, but was laughed at into the bargain.
What tempted you to change them?"

" Because I told you, over and over again,"
said the Baron, angrily, " that the guard-room
was no place to run the chance of playing
with false dice."

" Well, my master," said Jaques Maletot,
" there is no help for spilt milk ; so let the past
alone.   Baron, you fleeced the Cavalier Saligné
out of five thousand crowns last night;
whether he will pay you is another thing.
Here," taking up the paper the Captain had
been examining so attentively when they
entered the room, " here is an order drawn by
the Signore Leone Grimani upon a Bank in
Florence for the sum of ten thousand ducats,
the balance of a sum lodged with the said
Bank for the use of the Countess d'Alberti, who,
by the way, went by the name of the Signora
Erizzo.   Now the only difficulty lies in putting
the signature of your worthy father, and let me
alone for doing that.   Have you succeeded,
Captain, in getting an old letter of your
father's, to enable me to copy his signature,

which I will do so cleverly and exactly that he will swear it is his own ? "

" Now, I have another piece of news for you," continued the valet. " There is at this moment in your father's cabinet a casket of jewels belonging to the Marchese d'Obizzi, worth at least one hundred and fifty thousand ducats of Venice."

" The deuce there is !" exclaimed Captain Grimani, while the Baron rubbed his hands in exceeding delight ; " how did you contrive to get a sight of them—eh, Jaques ? "

" First let me get through that little business of the order on the Florentine Bank, because there must be no delay. I heard every word that passed between your cautious father, Captain, and the Marchese in two interviews ; and I can tell you, though I don't rightly understand one part of it—but this I made out—that the Marchese has lost some important title deeds and papers belonging to some great estates purchased by his grandfather from the family of the Contarini."

"Do you say so?" exclaimed the Baron, starting up; "then by Heaven! I will beggar this proud boy if that is the case, and fill our pockets at the same time."

"The devil you will," said the Captain, in a mocking laugh. "I have two words to say to that part of your scheme. By Jove! you forget that I am to receive ten thousand ducats the day he marries my sister; and I have no intention of letting her marry a beggar."

A very intelligent look passed between the worthy Maletot and the Baron. The latter seemed somewhat foolish at having so inconsiderately betrayed his feelings; however, seating himself, he said—

"What a dolt I was; I entirely forgot that circumstance; but let Jaques finish the affair of the order, for, as he says, it must be done without an hour's delay."

"By Saint Nicholas! if it is not," said the valet, "in a day or two the Signore Grimani will send an order himself, for he is preparing to settle with the Marchese their outstanding accounts. Now, I will take this order, and so well will I disguise myself that I can defy detection."

" There are two specimens of my father's handwriting, and his signature attached to both," said the Captain, tossing two letters to Jaques Maletot, " when you have done, let us hear about the casket of jewels—*one hundred and fifty thousand ducats!* By Jupiter! that sum would set us all to rights, eh, Baron?"

" Yes," cried the Baron, " but there will be some risk in getting at them."

" Not the least, Monsieur le Baron," said Jaques Maletot, looking up from his task. " I have the way and the means already prepared. You do me injustice by imagining for a moment that, living as I have done several months in the Signore Grimani's mansion, I should have neglected my opportunities. There," he continued, throwing the two letters and the forged document to the Captain;

"what think you of that? Won't you swear to the signature being your father's?"

"It's a curious bird that robs its own nest," said the Captain, making use of an Italian proverb; "but I know my father will not be made answerable for that sum, even if you get it. Yes, the signature is admirable; it would puzzle the old man!"

"Ah! That talent of mine," said the valet, with a sigh; "it lost me my mistress, and drove me into exile."

"And devilish near getting your neck into a worse noose than the matrimonial one you intended, and from which I saved you, Jaques," said the Baron.

"There is no good act without its reward," returned Maletot, laughing, and helping himself to wine; "you acquired the title of Baron de Chateauneuf by the transaction, while I accepted the title of valet to your Baronship. It is a curious world we live in."

It was strange that Antonio Grimani, with good blood in his veins, heir to a large fortune, holding an honourable title and situation, should enter into league with two such un-principled sharpers. Licentiousness, evil companions, great extravagance, love of wine, and a devouring thirst for gambling of every description, had in four years obliterated every good feeling and principle in his nature, and in the end, reduced by debt and evil passions, had warped and destroyed both soul and body. He leagued himself by encouraging the villanies of these two notorious French sharpers, who were deceiving him and leading him on by degrees—making him their tool—till they saw a fit opportunity, by a fortunate hit, to make their own fortunes, and leave him the victim.

The false Baron de Chateaunœuf, the younger son of a French officer, had been well brought up and educated, but by the death of his father was unfortunately left his own master at the age of eighteen ; his only brother, serving in the French navy, was abroad. Naturally wild and inclined to pleasure, Pierre le Grange, his real name, entering into the dissipations of Paris, soon became a ruined young man, and went on from bad to worse till he was obliged to quit Paris, taking with him, for companion and associate, Jaques Maletot, a finished and plausible villain. They travelled over many countries, living by play, false dice, and various devices, in all of which Jaques Maletot was an adept. At length they came to Venice; Pierre le Grange taking the title of Baron de Chateaunœuf, and Jaques calling himself his valet.

In the gambling saloons the Baron formed an acquaintance with the Lawyer's son, from whom the Frenchman found it no difficult matter to win large sums of money, and by degrees they fully understood each other, and in the end became associates in evil doing. The Baron found a very apt pupil in the young Grimani; and so well managed his part, that ere long he got him completely in his power. He then taught him how to win large sums of money, which rendered him still more extravagant and greedy of gain. Introduced into the domestic circle of the lawyer, other schemes entered the head of the crafty Frenchman; he next established his own associate, Jaques Maletot, as the valet of Grimani.

In the midst of his schemes of villany, the false Baron became desperately inflamed with a passion for Bianca Grimani—we will not profane the name of love by classing the feelings of the Frenchman for the Signora Bianca with that chaste and holy term. Specious, and to a certain degree pleasing in manners, and apparently, to her, a nobleman of rank, for he was ostentatious in his mode of living and dress, Bianca did not discourage his attentions till the intelligence reached her father of Ferdinando d'Obizzi's visit to Venice. Oh! gold, the bane of the human heart! Yet, what blessings does not its possession enable us to confer on those who have to struggle against adversity and poverty.

The love of gold, united with ambition,

swayed the heart and mind of Signore Grimani;
he at once conceived the project of uniting
his daughter to the young Marchese d'Obizzi;
and Bianca, equally ambitious of rank and
wealth, readily entered into her father's plans
for captivating the Marchese, though, at the
same time, she was greatly perplexed to know
how to manage matters with the Baron, with
whom she had gone a little too far. Alas! if
her brother's heart was a prey to the Evil
One, Bianca's was not quite free from stain.

CHAPTER VIII.

With an anxious and somewhat troubled mind, Ferdinando d'Obizzi put on his silver and blue domino, underneath which he wore a rich Spanish dress, as he intended accepting the Doge's invitation to the Ducal Palace, sending one of the servants of the Aquilla Nero to await his coming in the room appointed for changing his dress, &c. He was to meet the Signore Grimani, his daughter, and the Signora Pisani at the Palace.

It was rather late when the Marchese left the Hotel; he had dismissed his gondola, preferring to walk; the night was lovely, though the moon was not visible. The causeway from the hotel led along a similar one, upon which the mansion of the Signore Grimani was situated. Throwing a large mantle over his domino, he proceeded thoughtfully along the narrow riva till he came to a projecting wall, close to the back entrance to the Grimani mansion.

The rear of the lawyer's house opened on a narrow canal, the front upon a much wider one, leading into the Grand Canal. It chanced that the Marchese paused for an instant to adjust his mantle; during that moment, as he raised his eyes, he observed the small door of the lawyer's mansion open, and a man come cautiously out, who, looking along the canal, whistled in a low yet distinct manner.

The Marchese was at once struck by this action; for he was aware that the inmates of the mansion were never allowed egress through that door after nightfall, as, at sunset, the key was always brought and placed in the lawyer's study or office. Robberies were extremely frequent in Venice at this period, and since the burning of his office the Signore Grimani had been exceedingly particular. Standing in the deep shade of the wall, and enveloped in his dark mantle, the Marchese was unseen.

As the tall figure, muffled in a cloak, whistled, a gondola came swiftly up the canal to the side where the individual stood. The man dropped carefully into the boat a large bundle, and then jumped in. The next instant a second man came out through the door, carrying something that appeared very heavy.

With an active bound Ferdinando sprung forward, and with an iron grasp seized the man by the collar, exclaiming—

"Ha! villain; you are committing a robbery."

" By heavens, we are betrayed! " exclaimed the man held by the Marchese; who, drawing a stiletto from his mantle, made an attempt to strike his detainer, but, with a powerful jerk, the Marchese lifted him off his feet, and threw him prostrate on the causeway. As he did so, a heavy casket fell at his feet, rolling towards the canal.

This scene took place in much less time than in its relation. Just as the Marchese hurled the man upon the causeway, the person who had first leaped into the gondola, instantaneous as was the whole affair, sprung ashore, in his hurry discharging a pistol at the head of the Marchese without effect, while one of the men in the gondola, with a long boat-hook, strove to get the casket into the boat, but the Marchese had drawn his sword, exclaiming—

"Villains! you are mistaken," and kicking the casket a yard or so out of the way, parried the thrust of the stranger, who was masked.

A deep curse burst from under the mask as the man leaped back, and then jumped into the boat, instantly followed by the other, who had gradually crawled to the edge of the canal.

Intent upon saving the casket, which Ferdinando recognised at once to be his own, the robbers effected their escape. Not a soul was near the spot, for almost every individual was attracted by the festivities and illuminations in the Great Square of St. Mark. The gondola was rowed rapidly out of sight.

Picking up the heavy casket, though extremely astonished by the whole transaction,
the Marchese looked for a moment after the
receding boat, which he would undoubtedly
have followed, but he knew the causeway
turned off only a few paces on, where the
canal entered another and wider one, and the
fugitives could pursue their flight without his
having the power to follow, as he would have
to seek a bridge to enable him to cross the
canal.

Both the robbers were masked, but the
Marchese felt perfectly satisfied that the man
he first seized was no other than Jaques
Maletot, the valet of Captain Grimani. Passing in through the open door, he closed and
bolted it. He was now in a dark passage, at
the end of which was a flight of stairs leading
into the servants' hall. He called aloud, but
no answer being returned, he groped his way to
the stairs, and gaining the landing-place, again
called aloud. Still there was no response.
Rather startled, thinking some foul crime

besides robbery had been committed, he made his way to the kitchen, where, as he entered, moans and sobs caught his ear. There was a fire in the grate, and by its faint light, guided by the moans, he perceived two of the female domestics bound, gagged, and fastened to the legs of a ponderous oak table.

Throwing aside his cloak, and placing the casket on the table, our hero very soon released the cook and her assistant from the gags, their mouths bleeding from the rough manner in which they had been applied. The women were hysterical from fear and the joy at being released. When sufficiently collected, they procured lights, and, preceded by the Marchese, they ascended to the upper apartments, telling him at the same time that the three men servants and the Signora Bianca's two women had gone with their master and mistress to see the illuminations in the Square of St. Mark. They had been gone scarcely half-an-hour when, hearing a noise in the passage below, they went to see what occasioned it. Two men, masked, suddenly pounced on them, and extinguished their light; then, dragging them back to the kitchen, bound them securely to the oak table, and then proceeded to rob the mansion.

Ferdinando had his own thoughts; he felt convinced the second robber was no other than the Baron de Chateaunœuf, by his height and the tone of his voice, when he uttered his fierce execration.

The first place they went to was the lawyer's study; the lock of the door had been smashed to pieces, and on entering the room the handsome cabinet was broken open, though of great strength, from the interior of which the casket had been extracted. The papers and deeds it contained were scattered about, but the Marchese could not tell whether any had been taken away. The women kept up unceasing lamentations.

The party next examined the butler's pantry, the door of which had also been forced, and the plate chest broken open.

"There is no use," said the Marchese, "wasting time in examination. I will go in search of the police, and the Signore Grimani at the same time."

Placing the casket in a closet, and taking the key, he left the terrified women, and went out by the front door, promising to send home the other servants immediately. Desiring the cook and her attendant not to be alarmed, as the robbers would certainly not return, he proceeded with quick steps to the Piazza of St. Mark. As he went down the street he mingled with a great crowd of citizens, enjoying the brilliant illuminations of the street and the magnificent fireworks in the Great Square.

Ferdinando determined to enter the Palace and find the Signore Grimani, and tell him what had occurred, as he would know far better than he did how to proceed.

Passing up those magnificent stairs, called the "Giant's Staircase," and giving his name to one of the numerous ushers in attendance, the folding doors of the immense corridor were thrown open, and the Marchese, divested of his cloak, entered the crowded and splendidly-lighted saloons, opened for the reception of the better class of citizens of Venice. The scene was a singularly grand and striking one.

Before, however, we follow the footsteps of our hero amid the crowd, we must relate what occurred to the Signora Bianca Grimani after entering the Ducal Palace.

The Signore Grimani wore a handsome red domino, with a peculiar braiding on the sleeves, put on to enable his daughter or any other friend who might wish, to recognise him. The Signora Grimani and the Signora Pisani had on rich dresses of Genoa velvet, cut after the Genoa mode, and wearing long and graceful veils, the usual costume of the Genoese maidens of rank.

The Signora Bianca was somewhat depressed in spirits. She felt an unaccountable presentiment, a kind of foreboding of evil, which will occur at times, without our in any way being

able to account for it.   But Bianca *had* a
reason.   The last few days she had begun to
dread the Baron de Chateaunœuf; he had
made her a proposal that had roused all the
fierce resentment and haughty nature of her
disposition, and that proposal was " that she
was to marry the Marchese d'Obizzi, who
would unquestionably present to her a gorgeous
casket of jewellery, and then to desert her
husband, and carry off the jewels and anything else of value she had, and fly with him
into a distant land."   Oh ! how bitter was that
humiliating moment to the proud heart of
Bianca Grimani !   That he should dare to
make so monstrous and outrageous a proposal, left her for the moment unable to
reply.

Aware that she had encouraged his advances,
more for the sake of his supposed rank than
aught else, she bitterly repented her past career
in the doubtful and licentious society of Venice,
which would, perhaps, embitter all her future
life with sorrow.   Still the cool audacity of

the Frenchman to propose so vile an act to her, amazed her beyond bounds.

The Baron, however, made the offer to suit his own views; for he was quite aware that Bianca loved the Marchese, and that she would scornfully spurn his base desires. His own projects had been carefully planned, ere he made the proposal. He did it to wound and humble her, and vent the malice in his heart against her, as well as to show how completely she was in his power, and how, by a word, he could blast, for ever, all chance of her union with the Marchese d'Obizzi.

A scene of fierce scorn and passion on one side, and cold, bitter malice on the other, ended the interview.

Bianca threatened the false Baron with the just resentment of her brother, to which the Frenchman merely replied—

" I am not so easily ran through the body, as was your former paramour, the Count St. Felix !"

A passionate flood of tears, after the Baron

left the room, relieved Bianca's saddened heart, for with all her faults and follies she was guiltless of crime. She had fled from her father's house with the French Count, but instantly pursued and overtaken by her brother, who had not as yet fallen a victim to vice and dissipation, she was restored to her home, guilty of infatuated folly, but free from crime. This, probably, the world did not believe, for in general we are too prone to pronounce guilty those who err in judgment alone. Still, though this happened when she was scarcely sixteen, it left a stain upon her maiden name which neither time nor future good conduct could erase. Vanity and ambition were her ruling passions, and they completely smothered all the other kindly feelings in her heart.

Bianca's love, her pure, unselfish love for Ferdinando d'Obizzi, would, no doubt, in time have obliterated all the evil effects of her early education, had it prospered; but now, when she felt that her heart was truly devoted to the Marchese, she bewailed the past in bitter

despondency, for she dreaded lest he should
discover her first error, and consequently all
chance of a union with him vanish for ever.

Moving amid the gay and light-hearted
crowd, leaning on the arm of the Signora
Pisani, her eyes anxiously seeking to find the
silver and blue domino she knew the Marchese
was to wear, she presently whispered to her
friend—

" Look ! there he is !" and she directed the
Signora's attention to a tall figure she had been
so anxiously looking for.   The domino came
straight towards them.   He wore a full mask,
concealing all his features.   Bianca had understood the Marchese intended wearing the half-
mask.   The domino came to her side, and
bending down his head, said, in a very low
voice, which through the mask she did not
recognise—

" Dear lady, take my arm, and leave your
companion for a few moments."

Dropping her obliging companion's arm,
Bianca whispered—

"Go, seek my father; I will join you presently," and then, with a beating heart, she allowed the blue and silver domino to lead on through the crowd towards one of the saloons, where there was neither music nor dancing, and where the crowd was less dense.

Bianca felt her heart beat strangely, as she said—

"I have been looking for you, Marchese, for some time. I lost my dear father in the crowd very soon after we entered the saloon."

"Be not alarmed, lady," said the domino "though I am not the Marchese d'Obizzi."

A start of intense surprise, and a faint exclamation, escaped the lips of Bianca, as she strove to draw her arm from the stranger's, while she felt her cheek burn with the excitement of her feelings; but the stranger held her arm. They were close by a long range of ottomans, and no one near them.

"Bianca," said the stranger, "do you remember these features?" and raising the mask from his face, he bent a dark and piercing gaze upon her.

She raised her eyes, every limb trembling with excitement. As she met the stranger's gaze a wild shriek escaped her lips, as, with a deep sigh, she fell back in a swoon. A crowd instantly gathered round them. In a moment the stranger replaced his mask, and having caught her in his arms, placed her on an ottoman, saying to several ladies who had gathered round her—

"Give her air. I will bring water," and pushing through the crowd, he soon disappeared.

Fortunately, the Signora Pisani had followed at a short distance, keeping Bianca in sight. She heard the shriek, and saw the stranger place her on the ottoman. Much alarmed, she was soon by her side. Bianca's mask had fallen off, and her fair and beautiful face looked deadly pale.

The Signora Pisani begged some Signors

standing near to bear her friend to the balcony; the air from the open window, she said, would revive her.   Two masks, as nuns, carried Bianca to the open window, at the same time requesting the crowd to disperse, saying they knew the lady well, and they would take care of her, assuring them it was a mere fainting fit caused by the heat.

The fresh air blowing on the face of Bianca, she speedily showed signs of returning con-sciousness.   A violent shudder passed over her frame, and a sob, that appeared to convulse her, escaped her lips.   Her eyes rested on the unmasked features of the Signora Pisani, who clasped one of her hands in her own, while one of the other females held a glass of water to her lips, of which Bianca eagerly drank, and then her eyes roamed wildly over the persons of those near her.   In a few moments she recovered her recollection and her presence of mind, and, rising, thanked her friends, saying she had been completely overcome by the heat, and after a few words of congratulation

and other kind expressions, they proceeded
to enjoy themselves.

"What in the name of the Madonna,"
whispered Signora Pisani, " caused your fainting; and why has the Marchese d'Obizzi left
you in this strange manner?"

" Say nothing now, dear friend," said Bianca
in a low voice. " I am ill; get me home as
fast as you can, for I fear I shall faint again."

Much alarmed, the Signora Pisani supported
her through the crowd towards the outlet from
the saloon, and meeting an elderly cavalier,
with whom she was connected by relationship,
secured his services to look for their servants,
who were to be found in an ante-room set apart
for that purpose.

In a few minutes, wrapped in their mantles,
the friends left the palace, preceded by two of
her father's domestics with flambeaux, and
entering a gondola, soon reached their mansion.
They did not stop to look for the Signore
Grimani, but requested the Signora Pisani's
friend to find him, and tell him that his

daughter, feeling very unwell, had left the Ducal Palace to return home.

They reached the Grimani mansion about ten minutes after the Marchese d'Obizzi had left it. The door was opened by the two still terrified females the Marchese had left in the house.

"Oh! Signora. Oh! mistress!" they both exclaimed, as soon as the ladies entered the hall. "The house has been robbed, plundered. His lordship, the Marchese, caught the villains in the act. They had tied us to the kitchen table, cruelly cutting our mouths by gagging us."

"Robbed!" exclaimed the Signora Pisani.

"Robbed!" shouted the two domestics, turning pale.

"Where are the robbers?"

Bianca felt sick at heart, and whispered to the Signora, saying—

"Take me to my room, and send for my father. Oh! God help me. My lot in this life is blasted, destroyed for ever," and she burst into a passionate flood of tears.

Leaving the mansion of the Signore Grimani, we return to the Ducal Palace, and shall follow the footsteps of the Marchese d'Obizzi in our next chapter.

CHAPTER IX.

FERDINANDO D'OBIZZI's object was to find
the Signore Grimani, but in this he was not
likely to succeed, for the Signore, who promised
Bianca to seek for him, had found and told
him of his daughter's illness.   The lawyer,
startled at the intelligence, had hurried home
a few minutes before the Marchese entered
the Ducal Palace.

As Ferdinando continued his search, somewhat impeded by the various masks—some
stopping and bantering him on his evident
anxiety, as they declared, to find a fair frail
one, who had escaped his guardianship—a
mask in a rich Albanian costume took his
arm, saying—

" Ah, Marchese, where have you been up to
this late hour, for, by Jove, I have lost my
sister and her companion."

"You are the very person I wished to meet," said the Marchese, for the Albanian was Captain Grimani. Taking his arm he related, in a low voice, his adventure with the robbers.

A strange execration burst from the lips of the Captain, as he grasped the arm of the surprised Marchese, while he said, in an extremely agitated voice—

"Did you see their faces?   Have you any idea who they were?   Were they common robbers?"

"The sight of their countenances would be of little use to me," said the Marchese, thoughtfully ; "but I am satisfied that one was your valet, Jaques Maletot, and the other your friend, the Baron de Chateaunœuf."

"Curse their bungling—that is—by heaven, Marchese," continued the Captain, terribly vexed, "I am confounded and confused at such villainy. You must be deceived. At any rate I will go home at once, after calling on the chief of the police.   Stay you here, I entreat you, and find my sister and her friend. Do not alarm them," and without another word he hurried away.

Considerably astonished by the manner and strange words of Captain Grimani, the Marchese continued to slowly move through the rooms. Suddenly he beheld, close beside him, a tall figure in a blue and silver domino exactly similar to his own.

"May I request a few moments conversation with the Marchese d'Obizzi?" said the mask, in a low voice, close to the ear of our hero. "You will thank me, if you accede to my request."

"If this be any masquerade mummery," said the Marchese, "pray say so, for I have no inclination for any such amusement at this moment—I am engaged."

"I assure you, Marchese, it is not. What I have to say is important. Follow me into a distant saloon; the crowd is proceeding towards the supper-rooms, and we shall be unobserved."

Surprised, and perhaps a little curious, Ferdinando followed the stranger, and in a few
minutes they were in a nearly deserted saloon.

"Signor Marchese," said the stranger,
stopping, "I will say what I have to communi-
cate in as few words as possible.   You are
looked upon in Venice as a suitor for the hand
of Bianca Grimani."

"What mean you, sir," said the Marchese,
feeling the blood rush to his cheeks and
temples.   "People make very free with my
name, and play the spy upon my actions."

"They do, Marchese," interrupted the
stranger, "and you cannot prevent them.
Are you aware that Bianca Grimani, three
years ago, fled from her father's house with
the Count St. Felix, and that her brother
pursued the fugitives, and ran his sword
through the body of the said Count when he
was off his guard, and took his sister back?
Would you, Marchese d'Obizzi, marry the
paramour of St. Felix?"

So confounded was the Marchese, that he

remained for an instant unable to utter a word. At length he said—

"And pray, sir, in what light am I to look upon you for this gratuitous information, which, if true, is cruel and unmanly ; and, if false, deserving instant chastisement ?"

"If you are anxious, my Lord," returned the mask, " of being the lady's champion, and choose to give me the lie, I shall not baulk your inclination. To the first part of your question, I will answer you candidly. I give you this information, not from friendship, for I know you, my Lord Marchese, only by name and report."

"To suit your own views, then," interrupted Ferdinando, fiercely.

"Exactly so," returned the stranger. "You have only to ask the lady whether it be true or not, or enquire of any one you please in Venice, and they will enlighten you on this subject. I have done my part ; and to-morrow night, at the hour of eleven, I will be at the back of the church of Sta. Fosca, either to receive your thanks for saving you from a *mésalliance,* or give you satisfaction at the point of the sword, as you may please."

"And what guarantee," said the Marchese, in a troubled and vexed tone, "have I that you will meet me? You are unknown to me."

"That difficulty," returned the mask, dryly, "I cannot overcome; however, if you feel so deeply the wrong put upon the lady, as you think, follow me to the place I have named, and you shall have satisfaction beforehand."

Ferdinando, naturally of a quick temper, felt a strong inclination to do so, but restraining his passion, answered the domino, whose dark eyes through the mask never left their fixed look upon him—

"Be it as you propose; whether true or false, I expect to meet you to-morrow night at eleven at the back of Sta. Fosca."

"I shall not fail," returned the stranger, "and will not baulk your intention in any way. Good-night," and turning on his heels he passed into the other crowded saloon.

Ferdinando d'Obizzi remained some moments plunged in a train of very painful
thought. The events of the night vexed and
perplexed him. There were many causes for
vexation. He had associated with a swindler
and a robber. He had very nearly lost his
casket of jewels—jewels cherished as having
belonged to his unfortunate mother. He had
nearly, but not from love, linked himself by a
promise to a woman who, if what he had
heard was true, would have destroyed and
poisoned all the hours of his after life ; for
had he not been interrupted by the Baron the
morning he intended speaking seriously to the
lawyer's daughter, it is most probable, finding she really loved him, that he would have
bound himself by some conditional promise.
If what he had heard now proved true, he
determined, before ten days had passed, he
would leave Venice.

The hour was approaching appointed for
the private supper party of the Doge Contarini, and having been most especially invited,

he thought it only right, for many reasons, to
attend. Abstracted in mind, he moved on,
mingling with the crowd of maskers in the
room set apart for dancing, intending to seek
an usher to conduct him to the Ducal private
saloons. Just at this moment he felt his arm
touched by some one near him, in a marked
manner. He looked round, and standing close
to him was a female form dressed as a Priestess
or Votary of the Temple of Vesta.

"Fair domino," said the Vestal, "pause one
moment. I waited patiently till your con-
ference with your twin brother, as far as dress
goes, had ceased; and now you were nearly
escaping me."

"And pray, fair Priestess," said Ferdinando,
eyeing the graceful form before him—seen to
advantage in the simple but chaste attire of a
Vestal of the Temple—"what can I, a stranger,
do for you, for we worship not at the same
shrine?"

"Ah! your earthly devotion is woman,"
replied the Priestess; "and alas! you worship

a frail one.   But you are no stranger to me, Marchese."

Ferdinando was astounded. "How is this?" he thought to himself, "My disguise is a poor one ; or I am watched by those who seem to know me well, and yet I know nothing of them."

"You are surprised, Marchese," said the mask, in a low voice; "remain silent. This time it is a friend that speaks to you."

"I am indeed surprised," returned Ferdinando, "for I know few persons in Venice."

"Better," continued the Vestal, "that you had known less, and mixed, as your rank required, with your equals.   You would not then have thrown away your love upon a woman unworthy of you ; for Bianca Grimani some years back fled from her home with the Count St. Felix—bear that in mind ; we shall meet again," and a great crowd of maskers, retiring from a dance, separated them, and before the Marchese could recover from his surprise, the

Priestess of the Temple of Vesta was lost to his sight.

Perplexed, and a little confused in mind, and not a little angry with himself, he passed on, gained an antechamber, and accosting an usher, requested to be conducted to the Ducal Saloons.

" Follow me, Signore."

In a short time they reached a magnificent saloon, in which, however, there were only to be seen a numerous train of domestics, and four ushers with white rods. The man who conducted the Marchese called one of them, and confided our hero to his care.

" You will please, Signore," said this usher very respectfully, " to give me your name, and also to divest yourself of your domino and mask."

On giving his name, the usher turned over the leaves of a book lying on the table, saw the name, bowed, and closed the book, saying—

" Follow me, my Lord Marchese."

Passing through two other saloons, in which

were some thirty or forty gentlemen richly habited, the usher introduced our hero to a very distinguished-looking individual, the Count Lando, who had been appointed by the Doge to receive the guests invited to his private supper.

Count Lando was past the meridian of life, with a benevolent expression of countenance, a member of the Council, and the great friend and adviser of the Doge. He received the Marchese most kindly, shook his hand warmly, saying—

" I am rejoiced to see the son of my noble friend at last amongst us. Believe me, there are others that will welcome you. I heard of you, Marchese, but heard it reported that, for some reason, you wished to avoid society."

Ferdinando felt his cheek flush a little, as he replied—

" I certainly, Count Lando, did not express any such determination; but, as certainly, I refrained from mixing with the gay world from a feeling which at present I will not trouble you by relating, for I see by the opening of those folding-doors that we are summoned to supper."

"No, not yet. It is his Highness with his daughters, and the ladies in attendance. Excuse me for a moment."

Ferdinando stepped back with the rest of the company as the Doge and Duchess entered the magnificent saloon, which was brilliantly illuminated. While he was gazing at the splendidly-attired train of ladies that followed the Duchess, he felt his arm taken, and turning, saw his friend, Captain Grimani, very handsomely dressed in the State uniform of the Doge's Guard.

"All right, Marchese," whispered the Captain. "Police in hot pursuit of the rascals. Saw my father and sister; rather startled; the old man groans terribly for the loss of his plate, but excepting that, all is right. I heard that you had saved your casket—how fortunate!"

"It was indeed," returned the Marchese, very dryly.

chair, and advance into the circle. They were both young and beautiful, but the younger rivetted his attention in a remarkable manner. She was attired in white satin, with no other ornament on her entire dress or hair save a single chain of splendid pearls twined through her luxuriant brown hair. She was apparently not more than sixteen or seventeen years of age at the utmost. A visible air of timidity, and an evident wish to keep out of observation of the company, was very apparent, and yet no creation of the fancy could be more exquisitely lovely than the form and face of that young girl.

Ferdinando was standing sufficiently near to be able to distinguish the colour of her eyes, which were of a deep blue; and the long silken lashes and beautifully-arched brows were not to be surpassed. Her complexion was, for a native of the south, dazzlingly fair, and, though so young, her slight form was grace itself. The companion of this lovely girl was also very fair and lovely, taller and less slender. Some words dropped by a lady standing near Ferdinando, informed him who the elder of the maidens was. She was the youngest daughter of the Doge.

Just as our hero was turning to look for Count Lando, the great doors of the saloon were thrown open, and several ushers announced that the supper was ready. There was a general movement, and at that moment the Marchese caught the Duchess's eye, and a sign from her brought him to her side.

" I will confide to your care and attention," she said, in a low voice, " my daughter's young friend, to whom such scenes as this are quite new," and, without mentioning names, the fair young girl who had so fascinated his attention, was confided to his care. A rich colour mounted to her cheek, as, for an instant, she raised her lustrous eyes to his face, and then timidly placed her arm within his. The other nobles and gentlemen selected each a fair dame or maiden, and then all followed in the train of the Doge and Duchess.

" I fear, fair lady," said Ferdinando d'Obizzi,
" that her Grace, the Duchess, has confided
you to inexperienced hands, as this is the
first entertainment of the kind at which I
have ever been present."

In a sweet, low, musical voice, the maiden
said, with a blush and a smile—

" I suppose her Grace thought that being
both novices we should feel less embarrassment,
and mutually forgive each other any error of
etiquette we may commit."

" Mine was a very fortunate lot, Signora,
and I bless my ignorance of courtly ceremonies
if it has caused me this pleasure."

By this time they had reached the gorgeously-
furnished tables.   The whole service was of
gold, with the arms of the Republic engraved
on each piece of plate, for it was the State
service, not the private property of the Doge.

Notwithstanding his want of knowledge of
courtly forms and observances, the Marchese
managed to secure a place at the upper end of
the table for his fair and lovely partner.   By

degrees his gentle manner, as he conversed with the fair girl beside him, heeding very little indeed the sumptuous and luxurious edibles before him, won her gradually from her extreme timidity, and the two hours the supper lasted passed like magic. It appeared to his companion a dream, when the Doge and Duchess, and all the ladies, rose from their seats, and, after some words spoken by the Doge, which the Marchese did not happen to hear, for the best of all possible reasons—his eyes and whole thoughts were elsewhere—the whole bevy of beautiful women, his fair unknown in the midst, vanished from the saloon, and immediately after the entire party separated.

Before leaving the saloon, Count Lando accosted our hero, and after some remarks with respect to the entertainment, said—

" I trust, my dear young friend—I take the liberty of calling you so—that you will consider yourself a welcome guest at my palace. The Countess was not well enough to attend this fête, and my daughter kept her company, but she will, however, be delighted to receive you."

With many expressions of gratitude for the Count's attention, Ferdinando, with a slight hesitation of manner, said—

" I have a favour to ask you, Count. Pray, who was that fair girl the Duchess so kindly confided to my care for the supper? You doubtless saw the lady I mean."

" I did," was the reply, "and never did I behold, but once before, one so lovely. You were regarded with jealous eyes, Marchese, I assure you; but as to her name, I cannot enlighten you. I heard a lady say—for that beautiful creature attracted immense attention —she was the beloved friend and constant companion of the Lady Paulina, the youngest daughter of the Doge. This is her first appearance here. I did not hear her name. Take care, Marchese, yours was a dangerous situation to-night, or rather this morning, for the dawn is even now breaking," and pressing his young friend's hand, the Count retired.

Ferdinando having procured his cloak, proceeded to the Quay of the Piazetta, and, hailing one of the many gondolas in waiting, returned to the Aquilla Nero. He threw himself on the bed, but as to sleep it was quite out of the question. Were the thoughts that chased each other through his bewildered brain pleasing or happy ones? Far from it. Bitterly did he blame himself for the way he had acted since his arrival in Venice. He now discovered his error; he had kept aloof from his equals in rank; had devoted himself in a manner to one family only; and allowed himself to be introduced to a man who had turned out a common robber, a housebreaker, and was seen often in his company. In one sense he congratulated himself that no underhand persuasion of either the false Baron or Captain Grimani had induced him to visit either the Ridotto or any mansion where gambling was the chief inducement. But he had allowed himself to pay a somewhat marked attention to a lady to whom in reality—for he felt it now keenly—his senses, and not his heart, were engaged; and now, if the intelligence he had received from the unknown in the silver domino, and also from the Priestess of Vesta, was strictly true, what a dilemma he had brought himself into with the family of Grimani.

In the midst of all his troubled thoughts, the image of the lovely stranger, with whom he had passed the two happiest hours of his life, rose perpetually before him. Her sweet innocent expression of countenance, her lustrous eyes, her voice so clear and musical, had sunk into his heart in a manner strange and unaccountable. Then again, as he tossed and turned on his uneasy couch, his vow rose to his memory and filled his mind with a vague feeling of evil. The future appeared dark and sad to his young spirit, unlike his early years, when nought but the love of glory occupied his thoughts and mind. He sighed as he closed his eyes and tried to sleep, but the phantoms that floated before his vision in his waking, haunted equally his hours of uneasy slumber; but the most prominent of all was the fair young face of the unknown maiden, at whose side he had passed two very happy hours. Her sweet smile and look of perfect innocence seemed to soothe his troubled thoughts; and with this image before him, he at length sunk into a refreshing sleep.

We must now, gentle reader, leave the City of Lagunes and our hero, and in our next chapter turn to other lands and other characters, whose claims exercised a powerful influence on the subsequent career of Ferdinando d'Obizzi.

CHAPTER X.

On the coast of Liguria, some fifty odd miles
to the westward of Genoa, is the town of
Oneglia, built directly on the coast, and backed
by an extremely limited but beautiful country
—in fact a valley surrounded by ranges of lofty
and sterile mountains.   At the period of our
story, Oneglia was only to be approached either
by sea or by muleteers traversing the dangerous
and narrow paths across the lofty mountains
that intervened between it and every other part
of Italy; for the policy of the Republic of
Genoa at that time was to render every approach to the City of Genoa as difficult as
possible.

Towards the latter end of October, some five
or six years prior to the opening chapter of this
story, a large three-masted zebec approached
the town of Oneglia, standing in from the

westward under full sail. The day was both
bright and beautiful for the time of year.
Not a cloud obscured the fair blue sky, and
the water sparkled and rippled under the
influence of a gentle land wind.

The month of October is often one of the
pleasantest in the year on this part of the
Ligurian coast, sheltered from easterly gales by
a noble headland. The western boundary of
the Genoese gulf, protected from the north by
the great range of maritime Alps, Oneglia
scarcely feels the effects of winter, being far
superior as a residence than Nice, so subject as
it is to the violence of the north-west gales.

The zebec was a long, low craft, with
immensely lofty spars and sails, and light as
the breeze was, she approached the anchorage
before Oneglia very fast; for all these light
craft of the Mediterranean are remarkably
swift.

Walking the short after-deck of the zebec was
a tall and stately Signore, wrapped in a large
Spanish mantle of dark brown cloth; on his

head he wore a broad beaver, with a heavy
drooping plume of sable feathers. The masses
of hair, partly curled, that fell upon his neck
were tinged with grey. His features were remarkably handsome—though his age was full
forty-four and perhaps more—but their dark
and gloomy expression completely marred their
beauty.   Deep lines beneath the eyes, a
wrinkled brow, massive eyebrows, contracted
by habit, formed, notwithstanding the well-
formed features, a very repulsive countenance,
especially when the fierce flash from a pair of
intensely dark eyes rested on any individual
who might happen to look rather markedly
into his face.

Beneath the Signore's mantle, which at times
the breeze threw aside, he appeared handsomely, if not richly, attired; but carrying no
other defensive weapon than a heavy straight
sword. Seated on a bench near the tafferel of
the zebec was a lady, also closely wrapped in a
mantle lined with sable; she was younger
than her husband, for such was the gentleman

just described, by some eight or nine years; extremely fair in complexion, light brown hair, keen inquisitive grey, or light blue eyes, and very well-formed features, which, when in repose, looked extremely handsome. But there was a restless, uneasy look about her mouth, and a kind of nervous agitation in her manner. Resting its fair head upon her lap was a young girl of four or five years of age, with light hair, blue eyes, and fair complexion ; and playing about the deck was a sturdy boy, some eighteen months younger.

The water, though gently rippling to the breeze, and filling the lofty sails fully and well, was perfectly calm.

"So that is the town you speak of, Bertran," said the lady to her husband in a foreign accent, as he approached where she sat. "What is its name ?"

"Oneglia," he replied; "and a remarkably pleasing spot it is to look upon. Do you not think so, Amelia ?"

"Yes ; the little town looks pretty, peeping

out of those groves of evergreens and olives,
and the vessels drawn up nearly into the town
appear singular. But it must be a dull out-of-
the-way part of the world," and the lady
sighed.

"Where, papa, is the Castle we are going to
live in?" asked the boy, catching the heavy
mantle of his father, and looking up into his
sombre features timidly.

"Do not be impatient, boy; you will see it
in time," answered his father, rather harshly.

At this moment the vessel tacked, and
stood in to within less than a quarter-of-a-
mile of the shore, and then brailing her lateen
sails, let go her anchor.

"I will send our boat ashore," said the
Padrone, addressing the stranger, "for a larger
boat for your Excellency. The Castle of
Vachero is half-a-mile below the town. You
can see its watch-tower above that group of
trees. There is a landing-place under its
walls."

"Do so," said the stranger, "for I should

prefer landing with my family as near the
Castle as possible, and thus avoid traversing
the town. I sent my servants more than a
month ago, so that all is ready for our reception."

In less than half-an-hour a large and handsome barge was alongside the zebec, manned
by four oarsmen. Into this the Signore and
his Lady, the two children, and two female
domestics, and some travelling mails, were
placed, and pulled rapidly ashore. As the
party approached, they obtained a clear view of
the Castle of Vachero. It had, however,
nothing of the castle in its appearance, if we
except a lofty tower that rose from the cliff
beside it, and a kind of embattled rampart that
ran in front of the mansion, which was of
modern erection—that is, some five-and-twenty
years previous to our tale. It was a handsome
mansion, close to the sea; and its gardens and
evergreen woods rising up in the slight hill on
which it was built, gave it a very pleasing
appearance. It commanded a view over the

town, and a noble extended prospect to the westward. To the eastward the view was bounded by the lofty and picturesque Capo delle Mele.

The barge was seen approaching from the Castle, and several male domestics came down to assist. In little more than an hour the family of the Signore Bertran de Vengatelli were tolerably well located in their new domicile.

The Castle, some thirty years before the opening of our story, was built by one of the princely merchants of Genoa—Julius Cæsar Vachero—who rashly joined in a conspiracy of which he became the leader, to overturn the Government, massacre all the ancient nobility, new model the Government, and place it under the rule of the Duke of Saxony. But the plot being betrayed the evening before the intended outbreak, Vachero and many of his accomplices were arrested and executed. All his vast wealth was confiscated.

The Castle of Vachero was some few years

afterwards purchased by the family of Mar-
tineo, but, getting into difficulties, the Castle
was for sale at the period of the Signore
Bertran de Vengatelli's visiting Genoa.   The
Signore bought it, as well as the surrounding
grounds, at a very moderate price, and, as
we have stated, took possession of his
purchase.

The family of Vengatelli thus became the
proprietors of the Castle of Vachero some
four or five years before the events recorded in
our last chapter took place.   The first two
years of their residence in the Castle passed
over in great retirement and seclusion ; the
Signore never visiting the town, and no one
visiting the Castle.   His lady and children
sometimes rode about the country—that is, the
accessible part of it—for the valley was very
confined and the roads few and difficult of
access—she was, however, kind and willing to
aid any of the peasantry in her own immediate
vicinity.   Still there was an air of despondency
and gloom in the expression of her features ;

her only pleasure seemed to be in her children, for with her husband she was seldom seen.

Attached to the mansion was a chapel, and a padre from a neighbouring monastery officiated there, and received a handsome salary for himself, or rather for his brethren, who were only eight in number. The lady, her children, and domestics always attended the services, the Signore Vengatelli never. There was another individual forming part of the household, though he never associated with any of the members, save the Signore Vengatelli. This was his Secretary, a man of the same age as himself.

This individual was a person about the middle height, very robust, and with arms singularly muscular and very long. Though the same age as the Signore Vengatelli, his jet black hair and short beard showed no mark of the passage of time, no grey was to be seen mixed with it; his face round and full, the mouth small and the lips thin to a degree. His face might have been called well-looking,

were it not for the disproportioned length of
the upper lip; this, and the keen cunning
glance of his hazel eyes, left a very disagreeable impression on the mind of the beholders
as to the disposition and nature of the Signore's
Secretary. He entirely confined himself to
the library and private chambers of his master.
He was often absent for months, and their
letters to and fro were conveyed by private
couriers from Genoa, for in those days post-
offices were not established—at least in the
territories of the Republic of Genoa.

Time rolled on without much change taking
place in the family of the Signore Vengatelli,
except in the children; the little child had
grown into a tall, well-formed girl of some
twelve or thirteen years of age, and the boy a
stout, though not handsome, lad of ten.
When the Secretary was absent, many letters
arrived, and the Signore was uneasy and restless, his wife anxious and inquisitive.

At length, one morning, the Secretary, who
went by the name of Andrea Peretti, arrived

overland, having travelled on mules, which he changed several times on the road.

Let us follow him into the library of the Signore Vengatelli, who was pacing the floor with agitated steps, anxious for his presence. The instant the Secretary entered the room, and carefully closed the door, the Signore said—

" Is he dead ? "

" He is, my Lord Duke," said the Secretary, with a profound inclination of the head and a look of intense satisfaction.

The dark brow of the Duke, for such was now his title, for once looked free of the habitual frown it always bore, and a smile of triumph sat upon his lip. Then, indeed, an observer might have pronounced him eminently handsome. The traces of dark and strong passions for an instant disappeared, and even his years appeared less ; but it was only for a moment. His features soon resumed their usual expression. Still in his person and manner there was a visible change.

" I have better news still, my Lord," said

the Secretary, with a triumphant smile. "I have earned the reward I have for years struggled to gain."

"Ha? Then by all the saints," exclaimed the Duke, trembling with excitement, "you have found them."

"I have found *him*, my Lord," returned the Secretary, "but the Countess d'Alberti is dead!"

A savage scowl of bitter disappointment rendered the expression of the Duke's face terrible to look at.

"She has escaped me, then," he said, "and without feeling my vengeance. But you have found *him*. Sit down, and tell me from beginning to end how, after years of search, you discovered them."

The reader can very well imagine that in the Signore Vengatelli he recognised Bertran de Trevisano, by the death of his elder brother, Duke of Malamocco.

The Secretary sat down, while the Duke, leaning his head on his hand, his arm resting on the table, and his eyes fixed steadily on his companion, who proceeded with his narrative.

"You will be surprised, my Lord Duke, when I tell you that the Countess d'Alberti has actually resided for seventeen years within a day's sail of the City of Genoa."

The Duke made no remark, but his dark eyes flashed with excitement, and his lip trembled with emotion.

"When I left this castle six months ago to proceed to Venice, I embarked from Favona in a light felucca for Pisa. A violent and sudden gale drove us for shelter into the Gulf of Spezia. I intended pursuing my journey overland, but the Padrone begged me to wait till the next day, as the gale would surely subside. To amuse myself, I strolled through the place, and happened to enter the beautiful burial ground of the Dominican church, attracted by a party of workmen carrying a splendid monument of the celebrated Spezia marble to its place. Led by curiosity, I approached the monument, and remained astonished and be-

wildered when I read the name of the
Countess d'Alberti. The Sacristan was standing near. Accosting him, I said—

"'It is my wish to put a ducat or so in the
poor box in gratitude for my preservation from
shipwreck.'

"He seemed pleased, and, entering into
conversation, I learned that the Countess
d'Alberti, under the name of Erizzo, had
resided for seventeen years in a villa she had
purchased on the borders of the Gulf of
Spezia, and that her grandson, the Marchese
d'Obizzi—for their names and rank were at
this time well known, had served with high
honour in the Genoese fleet in their war in
the Levant—that the Marchese had set out for
Venice to resume his rank and station, but
that he still retained the villa, and left some
domestics in it. I was so amazed, my Lord,
that even the Sacristan observed my agitation;
but, placing a ducat in the poor-box, I thanked
him and departed.

"The Padrone of the felucca was right;

the wind fell, and we sailed the next morning. Having executed your Lordship's orders in Pisa, I proceeded as rapidly as I could to Venice. On reaching that city, I learned that your Lordship's brother had died suddenly, though, as you are aware, his illness was a fatal one. The Marchese d'Obizzi was in Venice, and had assumed his name and rank. There was a report, also, that he was enamoured of the Signore Grimani's daughter, a young lady who, some three years ago, eloped with the gay and handsome Count St. Felix, who was, I believe, a man of high rank, but small fortune, and a finished swordsman; and yet, it seems, that Captain Grimani, the girl's brother, ran him through the body and brought his sister back. Whether the Count died or not, I can't say. At all events, my Lord, the union of the lawyer's daughter and the Marchese d'Obizzi is openly talked of in Venice. He cannot certainly know of his intended spouse's elopement with the French Count."

" Did you hear from my lawyer ? " asked

the Duke, in a very thoughtful manner, "who was appointed guardian to my brother's two daughters, for as yet he has sent me no particulars with respect to them."

" You will have a packet by a private courier in a few days, my Lord, he bade me say. Why he would not entrust them to me, I know not."

" Humph !" muttered the Duke. " Strange ! Has Ferdinando d'Obizzi taken up his abode in his father's palace ? "

" No, my Lord, he has not. Neither has he taken any domestics into his service, but has a suit of apartments at the Hostel of the Aquilla Nero."

" That is very strange," remarked the Duke.

" There is another strange circumstance I heard while in Venice, my Lord."

" What is that ?" questioned the Duke.

" You are aware," said the Secretary after a moment's hesitation, " that your Lordship's brother's second wife was said to have died in giving birth to a child."

"So I understood," interrupted the Duke, roused from a reverie he was falling into. "You are aware that we never agreed, and that I was bound by an oath, which I took for various reasons, of which, also, you are aware, never to return to Venice whilst he lived, or assume my own name in any country I selected to reside in. I took this oath, and have kept it. He is dead: I resume my own name, and will set out, before the end of two months, for Brescia. But what is this strange rumour you heard?"

The Secretary coloured a little, and certainly hesitated, but at length said—

"It is rumoured, my Lord, that the Duchess did not die, but gave birth to a male child!"

With a savage oath the Duke sprang to his feet, while his eyes flamed with passion as he exclaimed—

"It is a lie! a cursed lie! It's impossible; my brother would have staked his soul for an heir; first, to deprive me of ever succeeding to the title and estates; and, secondly, to cut off

all chance of those accursed d'Obizzi succeeding to our inheritance."

"But your Lordship's son," said the Secretary, not daring to look the Duke in the face,
"will, it is to be hoped, prevent that taking
place."

A fierce laugh burst from the lips of the
Duke as he stopped, facing the Secretary, who
rose from his seat.

"This," and he half drew a jewel-hilted
poignard from his breast, "is a much more
effective method of settling the question. A
few inches of this will turn the tables.   The
young Marchese removed, the great estates of
the Obizzi become mine."

The Secretary's lips parted in a strange smile,
and his eyes glistened as he replied—

"That, my Lord, would settle the question
for ever, and save time."

"You are quite right, Andrea," returned the
Duke, with the smile of a fiend, "and it is an
instrument of which you well understand the
use.   But listen!   This deed must not be done

in Venice.   Mark me well.   When I hear of
his death, either by your hand or through your
means, ten thousand sequins shall be yours."

"Then the moment, my Lord, he leaves
Venice, his fate is sealed," returned the Secretary, in a bold and assured tone, while his eyes
met those of the Duke without flinching.

"We understand each other. Now, tell me,
Andrea, where you picked up or heard this
strange and accursed rumour of my brother's
wife not having died?"

"I heard it spoken of, my Lord, by old Pietro
Salvati, your brother's old steward of his estate
at Friuli.   I met him in Venice; he knew me
at once, though he was not aware that I was in
your Lordship's service.   The old man is living in Venice, and is very talkative."

"Then we must stop his talking," interrupted the Duke, savagely, "not that I believe
a word of the report."

"'I wonder,' said the old man to me, continued the Secretary, over a flask of wine,
which I knew he was always fond of, 'who

will be the Duke of Malamocco now?' and he
laughed, 'for I know something.'   I plied him
with wine, and asked him no questions.

"'Where have you been, Andrea,' said he
to me, 'since you left my old master's service.
You disappeared all of a sudden.'

"'Rambling over half Europe,' I replied, 'in
all kinds of service.'

"'And got rich in none,' said the old man
laughing.

"'No,' said I, filling his glass.

"'Well, it's a curious world,' said he, 'my
old master would have bartered his soul for an
heir to his title and wealth. He married again.
A young wife, aye, and a beautiful one, too.
Did you know that, Andrea?'

"'No,' said I, 'I have been absent so many
years.'

"'Ah! Well he did, though,' continued the
old man, 'he took her to Friuli.   They say
she died in childbirth.'

" Pietro Salvati shook his head, and after a
few moments continued, 'I think you have

made me drink more wine than I ought. But it's nothing to you or me ; but I know a secret ! There will be two Dukes of Malamocco ; but which is to be the right one has to be proved.'

"I could not get another word from him, and we parted. This is all the information I can give you on this subject, my Lord."

"It matters not now," said the Duke, "but I must get that old man into my power. I will try some other method besides wine to make him speak clearly. We shall then see who is the Duke of Malamocco."

CHAPTER XI.

In order that our readers may fully understand
the future development of our story, we will,
before proceeding further, relate briefly the
different incidents that took place in the career
of the brothers, the Count de Brescia and the
Duke of Malamocco, previous to the opening
chapters of this tale.

At the death of their father, the brothers were
left masters of great wealth in extensive estates
in Brescia, Padua, and in Istria. It was a period
when the nobility of Venice still possessed
enormous revenue sand great power. From their
earliest years no great affection existed between
the brothers, and in disposition they differed
as much as they did to personal appearance.
The elder succeeded to his father's title and his
estates in the Paduan territory and in Istria,
with   a   magnificent   palace   in   Venice.

The younger, Bertran, to the title of Count
and the Brescian property, a very considerable
one, having a magnificent castle on the
borders of the Lake of Garda.

The Marchese de Trevisano was of the
middle height, more robust than graceful,
with good features, and possessed of considerable talent and abilities, but in temper
he was imperious, and proud, to a painful
degree, of his birth and ancient name, but
scrupulous to a degree of the honour and
fame of his family name.

Early in life he engaged in State intrigues,
and his great abilities soon raised him to a
place in the Council; and shortly after he
married a lady of birth and fortune. Aware
of the strange will of his grandfather, his
ardent desire was to have male heirs, in
order that there might be no chance whatever of his estates passing into the family of
the d'Obizzi. This idea perpetually tormented
him, and the birth of his daughters and no son
had a great effect on his temper and disposi-

tion. Some years after he became a widower, and fourteen months after the death of his wife he married again; but all the particulars of this strange marriage were enveloped in profound mystery. For twelve months after his second marriage he lived in seclusion in a noble mansion he possessed near Istria. It was noised abroad that his young and beautiful wife died in child-birth—mother and children—for it was said there were twins—perished.

The Duke—for shortly before that event he had been created Duke of Malamocco, not alone for eminent services, but for the advance, if not gift, of immense sums to the exhausted treasury of St. Mark—The Duke, after the death of his second wife, mingled no more in the political intrigues of State, but retired into complete seclusion; and thus he continued till his death, leaving considerable fortunes to his two daughters, while his title and estates passed to his younger brother, Bertran de Trevisano.

We will now briefly touch upon some of

the incidents in the career of the Count of
Brescia previous to his succeeding to the title
and estates of his elder brother. Tall and
graceful in person, the Count of Brescia, with
remarkably handsome features and insinuating
manners, early launched into a terrible career
of vice and profligacy. His heart was the
prey of every baleful feeling; there was no
crime too bad that he would not commit to
gratify any selfish passion. A splendid swordsman, he gloried in insulting and afterwards
forcing the injured person into a duel, in
which he was sure to be the victor.

The Brescians became disgusted with his
notorious profligacies ; and tired of them himself, he repaired to Venice. At this period he
was only two-and-twenty. In so dissipated a
city as the " Queen of the Adriatic " he found
congenial associates. Nevertheless, a terrible
conspiracy, which took place shortly after his
arrival in Venice, forced him to quit it for a
time. In a year after he returned, and it was
during this second visit that he became pas-

sionately attached to Ellena d'Alberti, then considered the most beautiful woman in Venice. Infuriated and almost rendered a maniac by refusal of his love by Ellena, and learning that the Marchese d'Obizzi was the favoured lover, he lost all control over his fierce passions; he insulted the Marchese, fully intending to slay him. But this time, with all his skill, he was foiled, and received a severe wound that confined him for nearly three months to a sick chamber. Fearful were the vows of vengeance this violent and bad man took to be revenged on Ellena, as well as all bearing the name of d'Obizzi; and when recovered, and he learned that the Marchese was married to the woman he had vainly sought to win, his soul became a prey to the demon.

To recover his health completely, he retired to his Castle near the Lake of Garda, returning to Venice a short time after the Marchese d'Obizzi sailed for the Levant. It was then he planned and perpetrated the fearful murder of the ill-fated Marchesa. The child would also have perished but for the heroic grandmother. For this crime he was lodged in the dungeons of St. Mark, and brought to trial. His brother's influence at this period was very great; besides one of his family sat upon the Ducal throne. Before the trial took place he was visited by his brother, whose pride was tortured and mind distracted by the foul disgrace brought upon the name of Trevisano.

Bertran de Trevisano, with the fear of a terrible and disgraceful death before him, consented to whatever conditions his brother proposed. " I will save you from torture and death, and from confiscation of property," he said, " but you must endure a sentence of imprisonment as short as my interest can procure you. Two physicians will swear to your being insane at times. Now swear, that during my life, should your imprisonment expire before that event, you will not attempt to re-enter the territories of Venice, or assume your name and title, in any other land where you may wish to take up your abode."

After some argument and struggle of pride against the determination of his haughty and incensed brother, Bertran de Trevisano consented. The fortress to which he was condemned to be imprisoned for ten years was a building of great strength and vast extent, situated on the borders of the Adriatic. It contained a number of criminals within its walls, from thence they were shipped to the Venetian colonies.

In this fortress Bertran was allowed many liberties and even some luxuries—for what will not power and wealth achieve under such a Government as that of Venice, especially when it is considered that his brother became one of the dreaded Ten Rulers. Passing one day through the great court of the prison on his way to the gardens of the fortress, he beheld one of the convicts chained by the leg; the man's face was quite familiar to him. A second glance convinced him that it was Andrea

Peretti, once a secretary to his brother, but years back. Of all men Andrea Peretti was the one to suit the Count de Brescia in forwarding his evil passions and projects. A large sum of money procured the Count the attendance of the convict, who was condemned to hard labour for life for murder. During the ten years of his imprisonment this man continued with him, and devoted to him body and soul. Though a prisoner, the Count possessed full power over his property, which was managed for him by a lawyer and agents; and though unable to act himself, through Andrea Peretti, he found villains enough in Venice, the city of bravoes and assassins, willing and eager to undertake any crime, however horrible.

Did not sorrow or remorse for his past crimes, during the passage of those ten long years, enter the heart of Bertran de Trevisano? No; confinement and punishment only served to render his vile, bad heart more atrociously wicked; and in Andrea Peretti, a bold, astute, clever villain, he found a kindred soul. The

whole dream of his life was vengeance and a
fierce determination to destroy the son, as he
had cruelly murdered the mother ; Ferdinando
d'Obizzi he swore to sacrifice, as well as the
generous and kind-hearted Countess d'Alberti.

At the expiration of the ten years, Bertran was liberated, and with Andrea Peretti—
whose liberty he purchased—secretly passed
over into France, assuming the name of Vengatelli.   From Paris, in consequence of a duel,
he proceeded to England.   There he married
a lady of great wealth and beauty, for he lived
in great splendour.   Anxious, however, to
prosecute his schemes against the Obizzi, he
left England, and finally, as has been stated,
purchased the Vachero Mansion.   Peretti
traversed Italy, searching for the Countess,
but was always baffled, till, in the last tour, he
stumbled on her last resting-place

*   *   *   *   *

We must now change our scene and return
to Venice.   In the mansion of the Signore

Grimani, the morning after the masquerade, all was confusion and dismay. The lawyer was in a state of distraction and bewilderment on returning to his mansion, when informed of the robbery. Trembling with anxiety he hurried to his study. His secret cabinet was broken open, and its drawers ransacked. His first search was for the title deeds of which he himself had robbed his young client; they, and only they, were gone. Valuables he had none in the cabinet, only papers of vast importance. None were touched but those belonging to the Marchese d'Obizzi. Pale as death he fell back into his chair, the image of despair. Just then his son came in, looking confused and somewhat alarmed.

"Have you sent off the sberri in pursuit of those dastardly villains? You are to blame, sir," he fiercely exclaimed to his son, " to place such confidence in such ruffians. How could they have so deceived you ?"

Colouring highly, the Captain replied—

"They deceived you, sir, as well as myself.

How was I to know that this Baron was an
impostor, and my valet his accomplice."

The old man groaned, and hid his face in
his hands. Bitterly, at that time at least, did
Antonio Grimani curse his folly, not his
wickedness. He saw well enough he was the
dupe, the simple dupe, of his pleasant
acquaintances, and not for any consideration
would he that they were entrapped and brought
back, for they would assuredly betray him.
He had purposely misled the sberri to give
them time to get clear off; but he took care to
forward instantaneously a courier to Florence
to spare no expense, and to warn the bankers
to refuse any order presented for payment by
any one without a private note from his father.
By this he saved the money for his sire;
but that very *ruse* betrayed, in the end, his
own conduct to his parent.

In the midst of the confusion and dismay,
Bianca Grimani and the Signora Pisani returned from the Ducal Palace. They looked
miserably pale and heart-broken, and retired at

once to their chamber without heeding the terrible confusion they beheld, or even enquiring into it. Before morning, Bianca was in a fever and raving deliriously. A physician was sent for; the father requiring his assistance as much as the daughter, for this fresh misfortune completely overcame him.

Such was the state of affairs in the mansion of the Signore Grimani. The trace of the robbers had not been discovered, for the sberri were ill-directed, and were not made acquainted with the fact that the robbers were no other than the Baron de Chateaunœuf and Captain Grimani's own valet. The Captain let them know after he had allowed them six hours to make their escape.

Ferdinando d'Obizzi, after about two hours' sleep awoke. It was late in the morning, and the first thing he heard at the breakfast was the news, as the attendant meant it, of the robbery at the Signore Grimani's. He listened patiently to the man's intelligence, which certainly very much distorted facts. He, however, made no remark. He had scarcely finished his breakfast when Captain Grimani entered the room. He looked flushed and excited, and as he threw himself into a chair, said, with an oath—

"This is a monstrously unpleasant business, Marchese; how I could be deceived by that specious rascal, the false Baron, is inconceivable."

The Marchese felt that he coloured a little himself, for, to a certain extent, he had allowed himself to be deceived.

"I never liked him; I indeed suspected him of playing a part," said the Marchese, "but certainly never dreamed he intended acting the part of a common housebreaker. Has your father been plundered of much property, for I saw one of the rascals throw a large bundle into a gondola or skiff?"

"Only of plate and a jewel case," returned the Captain, "taken out of my sister's cabinet. We do not care for the loss. It is the unpleasant exposure of having received such a

swindler into our family circle. Pardon me
for asking you, Marchese, but how singular
that you came along that unfrequented causeway, and not—"

"Oh!" interrupted the Marchese, "that was
mere accident; I took it into my head, to avoid
the confusion of boats in approaching the
landing on the Piazetta, to walk.   I missed the
right turn, and came along the causeway by the
back of your father's mansion, and thus saved
my family jewels, which I would not have lost
for ten times their value.   They are now in a
closet of which I have the key."

Captain Grimani played with his sword
tassel, seemingly in a reverie, from which he
was startled by the Marchese calmly asking
him if he was ever acquainted with a French
cavalier—the Count St. Felix.

Captain Grimani sprung to his feet, his face
pale, and his manner singularly agitated.

"The Count St. Felix," he breathlessly exclaimed, passing his hand across his brow.
"What mean you, Marchese?" and from

being pale he became scarlet from the rush of blood to his face and temple. "Did you know the Count St. Felix?"

"No, Captain Grimani," returned Ferdinando d'Obizzi, looking steadily in the face of the agitated Venetian, "I did not. But I asked you. Did you know him?"

"I did," replied the Captain, with a fierce oath, and striking his sword-hilt. "He insulted my family, and I slew him."

"That you certainly did not," exclaimed a strong muscular voice, "worthy Captain Grimani," and the door, which was ajar, was pushed open, and a tall, handsome man, well dressed, in the Spanish mode, entered the room, holding his plumed hat in his hand; and then adding, "For, you see, here I am."

Captain Grimani fell back on his chair, as if struck by a pistol shot; his eyes glaring and almost starting from his head, fixed, as if fascinated, upon the intruder.

" This, then," thought the Marchese, gazing upon the Count St. Felix, " is my double; the blue and silver domino of last night. The plot thickens."

" You will pardon me, my Lord Marchese," said the Count St. Felix, bowing very slightly, " for this intrusion. I have been an inmate of this hostelry more than a week. Like yourself, I had a reason for dwelling here under a false name. Hearing that worthy Captain, as I passed the door, boast that he had slain me, I could not avoid easing his con-science by letting him see that, thanks to a very remarkable bad thrust, I still exist."

"Villain! I will slay you yet," furiously roared the Captain, springing to his feet, and rapidly drawing his sword he made a desperate lunge at the Count. But his arm was grasped by a power that mastered him at once. While the Marchese said, in a highly excited tone—

"Shame, Captain Grimani! Would you murder a man without a weapon in his hand?"

" Let him go, Marchese," coolly interrupted the Count, drawing his weapon. " He knows that I could kill him as easily as I toss this glove in his face," and as he spoke he dashed his left hand glove full in the Captain's face.

Captain Grimani became instantly calm, though his face betrayed the terrible conflict that raged within his breast. He spoke firmly and calmly.

"Enough, Count St. Felix; you have grievously insulted and dishonoured my family; you have inflicted on me an outrage that can only be washed out by the death of one or other of us. I am no match with you, I confess, with the sword; and as I am the party grossly insulted, I demand satisfaction to the death with no other weapon than the stiletto. You, Marchese, are witness to this insult and challenge, and thus I return your outrage," and suddenly catching up the glove he threw it forcibly in the Count's face, and rapidly quitted the room.

A mocking laugh burst from the Count St. Felix, as he contemptuously looked after the

Captain; and then turning to the somewhat amazed Marchese, he said—

" My conduct, Marchese d'Obizzi, demands explanation, and also what I said last night; for of course you have recognised me for the blue and silver domino."

" I will ask you a question, Count St. Felix," said the Marchese, sternly, looking the Frenchman steadily in the face.   " By what you said last night, Count, you have defamed the character of a lady with whom I have the honour of being acquainted. You said that lady was the paramour of the Count St. Felix. I say that is false !"

The Count St. Felix was some few years older than Ferdinando d'Obizzi. On hearing these words, his face flushed crimson, and his lips curled contemptuously, his glance roamed over the noble person of the Marchese, and then he answered, in a bold, cutting voice—

" After the language you have made use of, Marchese d'Obizzi, we must settle this matter otherwise than by words.   What I have said

I said, and will say again if you wish it. What I might have said, had you spoken differently, it matters not. I did you a service, you return it with an insult. I shall expect to meet you to-night, Marchese d'Obizzi, where I appointed. I shall bring a friend; you must do the same. Our weapon the small sword," and turning on his heel he left the chamber.

"Well," muttered Ferdinando, half-aloud, "I have been a little more than two months in Venice, and in that time have contrived to involve myself in a very entangled net. How this will end is doubtful. Though Bianca and I can never more meet, I will still defend her honour, which is, I feel satisfied, grossly slandered, and I will then quit this queenly city. But I must find a friend, and meet this singular Count St. Felix, and I know of no one I can request such a favour from except Captain Grimani, who, after all, I, in a manner, pity; for whether he fought fair or not, I cannot say. Still, it was to defend and punish his sister's betrayer; for, be it as it may, his design in urging her to leave her father's house was an evil one." So saying, he took his hat and left the chamber, and having his gondola in waiting, he proceeded to the Piazetta of St. Mark, and landing, sought the guard-room of the Palace, where he knew he should find the once gay Captain Grimani.

Two or three officers of the Doge's body-guard were in a noble saloon, chatting and laughing merrily; and looking out of the window was the Captain, who turned round when the Marchese touched him on the shoulder, and seeing who it was, looked into his countenance with a very troubled expression of feature.

"Will you favour me with five minutes' conversation, in private, Captain Grimani?" said the Marchese.

Without a word the Captain walked across the room, and opened a door leading into a smaller saloon, into which the Marchese followed him. When the door was closed, the Marchese, in a few words, explained the motive of his visit. Grimani's face brightened in an instant, and grasping Ferdinando's hand, he said—

" You are acting generously and nobly, and Bianca, who I am sorry to say is very ill, will acutely feel your gallant defence of her fair name ; for after what has passed, you will, I anticipate, never meet each other again. But this I can say, by my soul and sacred honour, Bianca is guiltless of all but folly and madness in flying with this Count St. Felix. She was almost a child at the time, not more than fifteen years of age. What his motive was in inducing her to take such a step, I know not ; but of this, rest assured, he is a nobleman of a high French family, and came here in the suite of the French Ambassador, and introduced by him to our previous Doge. Remarkably handsome and singularly fascinating amongst women, he earned what we cavaliers thought rather an enviable notoriety, As a swordsman he was unrivalled, and fought many duels, but in no case seemed desirous of

killing his adversary. I will say that much for
him. When I pursued him and my sister, and
overtook them between Fusina and Padua, I
attacked him at once, and he disarmed me; I
knew I was no match for him, and feeling myself justified, from the outrage inflicted on
my sister and family, in taking revenge on him
in any way "—the Captain hesitated and
flushed in the face, and then added, firmly—
" while he turned to look at Bianca, who had
fainted, I ran him through the body." The
Marchese started back with disgust visible
enough; still the Captain continued, " I
thought him slain, and carried my sister back
to Venice. We never heard again of the
Count from that day to this; of course the
event got abroad—at least the worst part of
it—and Bianca suffered more, perhaps, than she
deserved."

" I am of opinion," said the Marchese, after
a few moments' hesitation, " that taking everything into consideration, you, Captain Grimani, had better not act as my second in this

encounter to-night.   You are yourself engaged to meet the Count.   Would any one of
your comrades accompany me?"

"You are quite right, Marchese.   I am to
arrange for my duel with the Count to-night;
I will introduce you to Lieutenant Conrodin,
who, though only a lieutenant, is older than
myself by ten years.   He is an old and expert
swordsman, and quite up to these sort of
affairs.   I have seen you handle your weapon;
at the same time, let me caution you.   The
Count St. Felix is a cool and expert swordsman."

"Thank you," returned the Marchese, in
rather a cold tone.   "Will you give my com-
pliments to Lieutenant Conrodin, and say I
shall be happy to see him, and we will settle
the matter over a flask of Burgundy."

"He will be free at six o'clock, and you may
depend on his punctuality—a duel and a bottle
of Burgundy will be powerful incentives to the
worthy Lieutenant," said the Captain, with a
forced smile.

The Marchese then retired, certainly not with an increased regard for Captain Grimani. From the Piazetta of St. Mark, he proceeded in his gondola to the mansion of the Signore Grimani, and was shown into the study, where he found the lawyer alone, looking the picture of misery, occupied in counting over his papers. He could not look paler than he was, but he held out his hand to the Marchese with a nervous agitation.

"This is a terrible business, my dear young friend," said the lawyer, "but how miraculously fortunate that you saved your casket of jewels. No trace of the villains as yet. The whole of the affair is an astounding mystery."

"I imagine, my dear sir, it has been a very simple and long-planned business," returned the Marchese; "that rascally valet, your son was persuaded to take into his service, was only watching and waiting an opportunity."

The notion of the Marchese was a capital one, for every one was drawn, at that time, to the palace of the Doge.

"I am sorry to hear your daughter is suffering from fever."

The old man sighed heavily, saying—

"She is indeed ill. This business has affected her greatly."

"Here is the key of your closet, Signore Grimani," said the Marchese, handing the lawyer the key. "I placed my casket in it last night."

"You had better, Marchese, have the casket conveyed to the Bank of the Signors Vitubo and Goldo, where your moneys are lodged. After what occurred last night, I will not keep anything of great value in my house."

After a moment's pause, Ferdinando d'Obizzi said—

"Pray, Signore Grimani, can you inform me who, in case of my death, succeeds to my estates and property? I know that Trevisano succeeds to the estates, by right of my grand-father's strange compact! But he, if he lives, is out of the question; who is the next in suc-cession?"

Signore Grimani looked up with an air of surprise and interest, and after a moment's consideration, said, thoughtfully—

"I know of no blood relations on the father's side.   On the mother's side, I believe the Count Lando is the nearest connexion of blood relationship."

"And a very worthy and honest man he is," said the Marchese; "of high descent; not burdened with fortune, and a large family."

"I will not further occupy your valuable time, Signore Grimani," continued the Marchese, rising.   "I trust sincerely that your daughter will soon recover her health," and shaking the surprised lawyer by the hand, the Marchese d'Obizzi left the mansion.

Returning to the Aquilla Nero, he took pen and paper, and wrote for an hour.   He then folded the two letters, but did not seal them, and taking up a book, quietly perused its pages till the arrival of Lieutenant Conrodin.

CHAPTER XII.

AT the period of our story, the banking-house of Perugia, Malatesta & Co., of Florence, was one of the wealthiest in Italy ; and the Florentine merchants at this time were even rivalling their once powerful antagonists—Venice and Genoa.

One morning the Signore Perugia, while comfortably seated at his breakfast-table with his wife and daughters, was informed by one of his domestics that a private courier from Venice, who had travelled with immense speed, requested to see him to deliver into his own hands a most important letter.

" Show him into the next room," said the banker, and there he received the messenger, who handed him a letter, saying—

" Signore, I have travelled night and day with this despatch ; but, unfortunately, I lost a day in consequence of floods; nevertheless, I hope I am in time."

"You may retire, and refresh yourself," said the banker, and as the man left the room, he opened the letter, somewhat anxiously. As he ran his eyes over the contents, he gave a start, and a sharp exclamation, followed by the words—

"St. Antonio! There is no time to be lost;" and calling for his hat and mantle, the Signore Perugia, who was both short and fat, and somewhat limited in wind, hurried out of his mansion, and made the best of his way through the crowded streets to his counting-house or banking establishment, muttering sundry ejaculations of surprise and anxiety on the way.

On arriving at his office, somewhat flurried, he found one of his partners quietly reading a letter just received. As the Signore Perugia was out of breath, the Signore Malatesta spoke first.

"Here is a polite note from a Baron de Chateauneuf, saying—"

"What!" interrupted the Signore Perugia, recovering his breath. "You have not paid him, I hope."

"No, not yet," quietly replied his partner, wondering at the stout Signore's agitation. But the words "not yet" had a soothing effect; they restored the Signore Perugia at once, and he broke out into a hearty laugh.

"The office was not open," said the Signore Malatesta "when the Baron called; and he wrote a polite note, saying he had an order for ten thousand Venetian ducats on our house, signed and drawn by the worthy Signore Grimani: and that, having to leave Florence at midday, he would call in an hour."

"Tomasso, come here," returned the Signore Perugia, hastily. "Run as quick as you can, and tell Signore Baracco to send two of the secret police with you, and mind take them into the little saloon next our office of payment. They are to take into custody whoever I introduce into the room. Stay; better write a line," and taking up a pen, he wrote a few hasty lines, gave the letter to the clerk, who hurried off with it, amazingly curious to know what was wanting with the secret police.

"God bless me, Perugia!" exclaimed the Signore Malatesta, "what is all this about; you quite puzzle me."

"Soon unpuzzle you, *amico*," returned the banker. "The Baron de Chateaunœuf—ha! ha! ha! not bad! a Baron, too. He has robbed and plundered the house of Signore Grimani; stolen all his plate, jewels, &c., and has a forged note on our house for ten thousand ducats. Read that, for I am out of breath," and he handed the letter he had received to his partner.

"By Jupiter! Here's an escape! This letter is written by Captain Grimani, the worthy lawyer's son. He says his father is knocked all of a heap—a military expression, I suppose—and that this Baron has an accomplice—a Frenchman also—I wonder if he will come with the Baron. They must be sent to Venice."

"I wonder what they have done with the

jewels and plate? Doubtless sold them to some Jew pedlar by this time," said the Signore Perugia.

In less than ten minutes, two of the secret police, well-armed, though habited as simple citizens, were stationed in the little saloon; and in less than five minutes more the Baron de Chateaunœuf, extremely well-dressed, and with a perfectly self-possessed air, entered the large and handsome chamber devoted to the business of the banking establishment of the firm of Perugia, Malatesta & Co.

" Sorry to be so troublesome, Signore," began the Baron, " in calling on you so early, but the fact is I am much pressed for time, having an action of vast family importance now pending in the Courts at Paris, requiring my personal attendance."

The Signors Perugia and Malatesta returned the Baron's salutation with great politeness, and took the order presented, and read it carefully over.

" Quite correct," said the Signore Perugia,

handing the order to his partner, "and how will you take the money, Baron. Would an order on a Paris banker be convenient?"

"Let me see," said the Baron, quite coolly. "No, I fear, for certain reasons, it would not. If quite convenient, I will take it in gold. I have brought my valet to carry it."

"Oh, you have," returned the banker, "very well. Will you please, Baron, to follow me into my office of payment; and do you, Tomasso, call the Baron's attendant."

The Signore Perugia threw open the door of the small saloon, and, with a low bow, begged the Baron to enter. The Frenchman, with a salutation to the banker, entered the saloon, and in a moment was firmly grasped by the collar by two powerful men.

"So," said the Baron, perceiving that any struggle would be useless, after eyeing the two police agents. "So, I am a prisoner; and pray, Signore Perugia," he said, turning to that gentleman, who was rubbing his small fat hands, and smiling very facetiously, "on what

charge have these gentlemen laid violent hands
on a French nobleman ?"

"Signore," said the voice of the clerk, "the
Baron's valet is not to be seen anywhere."

A smile of satisfaction passed over the
features of the false Baron.

"If you are a French nobleman," said the
banker, with a look of dissatisfaction on hearing of the non-appearance of the valet, "you
have a strange method of employing your
leisure hours. There is a letter of Captain
Grimani's—"

"Ha! the villain!" exclaimed the Baron.
"I beg pardon, Signore Perugia, for interrupt-
ing you." The banker bowed involuntarily,
coloured, and then went on—

"This letter accuses you of committing a
robbery in the house of the Signore Grimani;
of carrying off plate and jewels; and having
in your possession a forged order for ten thousand ducats purported to be signed by the Signore
Grimani, and which I hold in my hand."

"Those are very serious charges," said the

Baron, quite coolly, " but they must be proved. In the meantime, gentlemen, you are squeezing my throat in an unpleasant manner, and causing me to cough more unpleasantly still."

Seeing the prisoner quite calm and behaving so very well, the two police agents relaxed their grasp a little ; as they did so the Baron — being, as we have said, a very powerful man — with a sudden and tremendous swing back of both arms, tumbled both police agents violently on the floor.

Before the amazed Signore Perugia could stir, he felt himself lifted up and pitched on the top of the two policemen. The next instant the Baron rushed through the door, locking it, and taking the key with him. One only of the clerks had the presence of mind to make a rush at the Baron, for which exertion of his intellects he received a tremendous blow in the face, which drove him violently against the stomach of the Signore Malatesta, who roared murder at the top of his voice, whilst a succession of blows and kicks were thundered at the door of the saloon by the caged inmates.

"You have killed me, Tomasso," groaned the Signore Malatesta, "with that blow you gave me in my stomach."

"I gave you!" roared the clerk, the blood streaming from his face. "Curse the villain, he has smashed the bridge of my nose; he has a fist like a sledge-hammer, and he has escaped. Yes, confound him, and locked the street door."

Great was the confusion and great the uproar without and within. A considerable time elapsed before the doors were burst open. There was a great crowd without, wondering at the uproar within. As soon as the doors were opened the two policemen rushed out, mad with rage, and set off to seek assistance, and hunt the city for the fugitives.

With his hand applied to the tender part of his body, the Signore Malatesta looked at his partner, who was rubbing his fat legs with singular vigour.

"That villain has nearly killed me. Here's a pretty morning's work," said the Signore Malatesta.

"By Jove he has knocked a piece out of my shin, and my legs are a mass of bruises," returned the Signore Perugia; "but, confound him, we have saved the ten thousand gold ducats. The police will catch the villain in half-an-hour."

"May the devil—the saints pardon me," groaned the Signore Malatesta. "I have an awful pain here."

"I should like to know who will pay me for the bridge of my nose?" groaned the clerk.

In the meantime, the Baron having locked the door of the counting-house, proceeded through the short hall and an open door, and walked coolly into the street, He did not hurry himself till he came to the labyrinth of narrow, crooked streets at the back of the Palace; then he quickened his pace, dived down a peculiarly deserted street, and entered an open door; mounted a flight of steps, and pushed open a second door, and there beheld a man very diligently emptying a large bag. He turned rapidly round, and seeing the Baron, exclaimed, with a look of wonder, "The devil!"

"Not exactly, Jaques Maletot; but it was near being the devil to pay. How came you to get out of the way? Curse that Captain Grimani! I will pay him off yet."

"Ha! So it was the Captain, was it?" returned Jaques.

"How came you to suspect anything?" again demanded the false Baron, beginning to strip off his dress.

"Why you see," said Jaques, "I am always suspicious when about a job of that sort. So when you went into the room, I applied my eye to the round piece of glass in the door—I saw you give the order—and I saw the glance the banker gave to his partner while you were looking another way. The look startled me; and when I saw him usher you into another room, and saw him make a sign to the clerk, and tell him to go and bring in your excellent domestic, I thought it better to make myself invisible. So we have lost the ten thousand ducats? How the devil did a messenger get here before us?"

"Quite easy," said the Baron. "We lost eight hours at the Ferry by the swamping of the boat, and nearly as many waiting for mules. Now, never mind the ten thousand ducats : we have what will bring us five times that amount. We must get back by a circuitous route to where we left our spoil, and we must get out of this place as quickly as we can. So turn out our intended costume of the Quack Doctor and his Merry Andrew. It is lucky that you compounded that universal balm last night— did you get the trumpet?"

"All ready, Doctor," and the valet laughed.

"Where is our host?"

"Gone out to change the ducats."

In a few seconds the contents of a large bag were turned out on the floor, and in less than ten minutes a most extraordinary transformation took place in the *ci-devant* Baron and his valet. A full curled wig of red hair covered the Baron's dark locks; a purple satin coat, laced with silver, a little tarnished, a very long species of waistcoat of white satin, edged also with lace, a pair of red plush hose fastened at the knee, a pair of white silk stockings, and a pair of shoes with enormous buckles over the instep, completed his costume of a Quack Doctor of the 17th century; added to which were a huge pair of false moustachios, red, like the wig, having sacrificed his own handsome black ones; a three-cornered cocked hat covered his head. He then applied a long, narrow, black patch over a part of one cheek and across the bridge of his nose.

"I think I shall do, Jaques, eh?" said the Baron, surveying himself in a broken mirror.

"*Sacre diable!*" said the valet, trying on a dress very much resembling a Harlequin's, only made of many-coloured cloths cut in strange forms; whilst one leg was clothed in blue and the other in red. A dark wig covered his light hair, and a curious cloth cap with three tassels ornamented his head. "*Sacre diable!* Monsieur le Baron de Chateaunœuf, I think it

would bother his Satanic Majesty to detect us.
Here is the trumpet.   I can blow a blast that
would rouse the ' Seven Sleepers.'   Ah !   If I
had not lost the trumpet we had when we
gulled the wiseacres at Padua, I'd astonish
them.   Well, we must keep this disguise till
we get back to our haunt.   Ah ! here's Jacob,"
and a meagre, miserable-looking Jew, with a
long dirty beard and unwashed face, entered
the   room.   He   grinned   and   rubbed   his
withered hands when he saw the transformation that had taken place, and his eyes were
fixed on the garments they had taken off.

"They are your perquisites, Jacob," said the
Baron, "in lieu of the score of small bottles
you supplied us with,   Perhaps you will taste
our invaluable balm before we go."

" Father Abraham forbid," groaned the Jew,
eagerly collecting the garments.

"You must keep them carefully hid for
awhile, Jacob," said the Baron, "for there's
sure to be a hunt for me through the City."

"Ha! ha! ha!" chuckled the old man.

"They will never see these again in this city; but here's the change I got for the Venetian ducats."

"Very good. Now let me see that our box is all right," looking into a small, neat case, with a stout leather strap. It contained over a score of small bottles, filled with a clear liquid, and some fifty or more red papers tied with blue silk, and a few pill boxes.

"Come," said the Baron, "this is all very well arranged; quite as good an assortment as physiced the good people of Brescia and Padua."

"Now, then, Jaques, don't blow your trumpet till you reach the Square, and then let us go out through the Pisan gate. Take another blow close by the gate, so that we may have a keen inspection of who is standing there."

In a few minutes they had traversed the narrow street and entered the Square. The Doctor with a huge cane, with an enormous gilt knob, strutting along in front, his Merry

Andrew following, to the infinite delight of a crowd of idle persons who followed their steps.

On reaching the Square they stopped. A kind of stand was made by opening three cross sticks, and on this the famous box of medicines was fixed. Jaques Maletot, then placing his trumpet to his lips, blew a blast, as he promised, quite sufficient, if not to rouse the Seven Sleepers, to confound any human being with the faculty of hearing.

Quack Doctors and Mountebanks were quite the rage at this period; they paraded the Italian cities, some of them with extraordinary pomp.

A considerable crowd of men, women, and boys began to collect, and Jaques Maletot, mounting on the top of a pedestal near, cleared his throat, gave another blast that caused the hearers to clap their hands to their ears; and then began, in excellent Italian, but with a foreign accent—

"Signoras and Signors. Permit me to announce to you the arrival of the great

Doctor Bombadino Stromboli in your beautiful
City of Florence, known all over the universal
globe as Fiorenza la Belle."

The people clapped their hands and shouted.

"This great Doctor—behold him!" The
Doctor looked superb. "He is just come
from the East; from the Turkish city of Con-
stantinople, where he has cured of the plague
no less than twenty millions—"

"Thousands, rascal," roared the Doctor,
applying his cane to the back of the speaker.
"Good people, I do not wish to arrogate to
myself undue praise—thousands, rascal. Go on."

"I beg pardon," began again Jaques Maletot, making hideous faces at his master's back.
"Twenty thousand people, and with one universal medicine ;   the great and glorious balm,
compounded, Signoras and Signors, of nothing
but herbs, gathered in the far East, under the
influence of the Moon, the Great Bear, and the
Planet Venus, diluted with the pure water of
the Nile, procured by the Great Doctor himself ten thousand miles—"

"Hundreds of thousands, rascal," roared the Doctor. "You must be taught better arithmetic."

"Well, it's not much difference," grumbled the Merry Andrew, "ten hundred miles from its entrance into the sea, at Jerusalem—"

"Villain, at Alexandria," interrupted the Doctor.

"It is the same water still," persisted the Merry Andrew. "The water of the Nile uncontaminated by reptiles; free from the whale and the alligator—"

"Hold your tongue," cried the Doctor, taking up a small bottle, and clearing his throat. "The cost of this small bottle to you, my good friends, will be only a half-florin, though to compound and collect the materials from which it is made, cost me years of trouble and travel. It not only cures the plague which, I am sorry to say, advances towards us rapidly, but its other virtues are numerous. It is to be taken only two drops at the time, its power is so great—that is at first; you then increase the dose to four, six, and finally, a whole bottle. It cures lumbago, the ague, palsy, toothache—"

"How do you use it for the toothache?" roared a big, stupid-looking peasant, with a prodigious nose.

"Quite simply," said the Doctor. "Most physicians, my worthy friends, would tell you to apply the liquid to the tooth. This is a false doctrine, I contend. The tooth is the seat of the disease; the thing is to draw the pain from the tooth. Dip a little liquid on a piece of lint on this incomparable balm, and then, at night, mind you, apply it to the tip of the nose; the pain is thus drawn to a part that has no feeling."

"By St. Nicholas!" cried the Merry Andrew, "I doubt that about the nose, master;" and suddenly he caught the huge knob of the peasant's nose, and gave it an unmerciful twist. The man roared murder, and Jaques blew a blast that stifled his roars and the laughter of the crowd.

"Come, come, Doctor, you must move on,"

said a man in citizen's attire, and whom the Baron recognised as one of the identical police agents he had upset in the morning, "the Grand Duke is coming this way."

The Doctor bowed graciously, but nearly half his stock was purchased before he moved on, which he then did, and stopped not till he came to the Pisan Gate, where he paused and made another elaborate speech, sold all his pills as sure charms, and lots of his powders as a most quick and effective cure for the colic. He then made a parting bow, and moved out through the gate.

The Doctor and Jaques Maletot had not gone more than fifty yards before they were overtaken by the gatekeeper.

"Pardon me, Doctor," said the man, "but my wife is doubled up with a fearful colic. What am I to do? Here are two florins."

"This," said the Doctor, giving him two of his red powders, "will cure her in one minute; but first get a flat stone, make it red hot, and place it on the part—mind you—opposite to the seat of pain, for counter-irritation, my friend, is the way to cure all diseases. Then put those powders in a small glass of water, and let her swallow them at once. Depend on it she will never complain again."

The man seemed rather astonished.

"What," said he, "place the hot stone on—"

"Certainly, my friend," interrupted the Doctor gravely, "my practice is different from all others."

The man bowed, and hurried back to his wife.

Whether the Doctor's remedy succeeded or not we cannot say. The red powder was cayenne pepper.

The two swindlers pursued their way without molestation to the next village; there they procured mules, and proceeded to Pisa. Here again they changed their attire, carefully packing up their charlatan costumes, which had often before served them in their schemes. There we must leave them, and certainly without any regret, wishing we had nothing more to say as to their future career; but as they must again appear, we take leave of them only for a time.

CHAPTER XIII.

It was a singularly bright and moonlight night in Venice; scarcely an air wantoned over the surface of her Lagune, or over her hundred water streets.   Deep shadows stretched across the Grand Canal, caused by her mighty palaces. No lamps of oil or gas lit up their narrow causeways, or rivas, where the rays of the moon peered not.   No buzz of human voices, no rumbling of carriages or carts disturbed the stillness of that city of the waters.

It was not the season of the year when the gay Venetian passed half the night paddling over the canals.   No, the air was cold; it was the month of November, and the hour was late; all was still, as if no tens of thousands dwelt therein.   At the back of the Chiesa San Francesco della Vigna there was a broad, open space intervening between the high blank wall

of the church, and the narrow canal that
formed an angle of the platform.   There were
no habitations for some hundreds of yards, for
the great church wall extended right and left
for a considerable distance.   On this platform
the moon's beams fell as bright and clear
almost as noonday; every object was beautifully distinct, for the moon being full on it,
not a shadow rested upon the platform.

Presently, as the great bell of the Campa-
nella of St. Mark tolled the midnight hour,
two tall figures turned the right-hand corner
of the old wall of San Francesco della Vigna,
muffled in large mantles; and almost as
punctually two other figures, also cloaked, came
round from the left, and both parties met on
the platform, and saluted each other, if not
cordially, at all events politely.

As the Marchese d'Obizzi threw off his
cloak, so did the Count St. Felix, for they were
the principals—the seconds threw aside theirs,
and then, with some surprise, both the Marchese
and Lieutenant Conrodin perceived that the

second of the Count St. Felix was no other
than Count Contarini, the only son of the
Doge, a tall, handsome man of some seven or
eight-and-twenty years of age.

Everything being arranged between the
seconds, and the combatants placed with a fair
regard to light, the Marchese d'Obizzi dropped
the point of his sword, and said, in a calm,
steady voice, addressing the seconds—

"This gentleman, the Count St. Felix, has
asserted that the Signora Bianca Grimani was
his paramour, which foul slander I declared to
be a lie; and I now stand here to maintain to
the death the truth of my assertion. Should
it be my fate to die, I wish you, gentlemen, to
observe, should these be my last words, that as
I hope for salvation, I do most solemnly
believe the assertion I have made to be most
true."

While the Marchese spoke, there might be
seen a slight degree of nervous agitation in the
features of the Count St. Felix. He seemed
to press his lips hard, and the hand that held

his sword was slightly agitated. However, as
the Marchese ended, he said, in a sharp tone—

"Let us waste no more of that chaste lady's
light," pointing to the moon, "for in ten
minutes she will be behind the Campanile of
St. Mark, and our shadows may obstruct us."

"Ten minutes," returned the Marchese,
coldly, "will be quite enough for our purpose."

"Ha! say you so; then have at you, my
Lord Marchese," and the same instant the
swords crossed.

Five minutes passed in a splendid exhibition
of steel; and then the Count Michale Contarini muttered between his teeth—

"The Marchese is right."

At the same moment, Ferdinando d'Obizzi
parried with wonderful skill a most dangerous
feint of the Count St. Felix; and the moment
after, his weapon, gliding under the Count's,
passed through the fleshy part of the right
shoulder, coming out at the back, the hilt,
with the power of the blow, striking against
the shoulder of the Count, causing him to

fall back a pace or two.   Ferdinando d'Obizzi
drew back his weapon, while the Count St.
Felix dropped his right arm, taking his sword,
while Contarini advanced to support him.

"I thank you, my lord, I can stand well
enough; but the fighting part of this evening's
amusement is over; for though I can use my
sword with my left hand nearly as well as my
right, I candidly confess it would be a mockery
to do so with the Marchese d'Obizzi, who is,
without exception, the best swordsman I ever
met."

"Count St. Felix," said the Marchese, "I
know not how it is, but I somehow fancy you
too much a man of honour to maintain so
cruel a slander upon a poor defenceless girl,
who certainly committed a rash act, but which
assuredly did not end in guilt.   Shall our
quarrel end here, or be continued, when you
are cured of that sword thrust, to the death?"

The two seconds had stripped the arm, and
bound a band across to stay the effusion of
blood, which appeared somewhat considerable.

The Count St. Felix hesitated for a moment; his face was pale, but in a steady voice, said—

"You have acted generously, Marchese d'Obizzi, for I know too much of the small sword not to be aware that when I made that lunge, if it was parried, my life was in your power. You changed your aim, and contented yourself with disabling me. I, therefore, now before these two gentlemen, solemnly declare that what I asserted against the honour of Bianca Grimani was totally without foundation; and if, Marchese, you will favour me with half-an-hour's conversation to-morrow, I will explain to you the reason—a bad one, I confess—that caused me to act as I did," and holding out his left hand, it was cordially pressed by the Marchese.

The whole party then assisted the Count to his gondola, and as he and the Marchese were located in the same hotel, they returned together. The Count Contarini, declining to accompany them, pursued his way to the Ducal

Palace on foot, after a moment's private conversation with the Count St. Felix.

The next day the Count's wound was stiff
and much inflamed, and the surgeon insisted
on his remaining perfectly quiet. The Marchese, therefore, would not allow him to exert
himself to talk, and deferred any explanation
till he was free from fever.

The Signora Grimani was still suffering
severely, and the old lawyer was in a confused
state of mind. The Marchese disliked the
manner of Captain Grimani. In a thought-
less way, he let slip the real feelings of his heart,
and Ferdinando d'Obizzi could easily perceive
that the Captain was sorely vexed that he had
not slain the Count St. Felix, when he had it
in his power. The Marchese did not disguise
his disgust from the Captain, and left him,
after a very short interview; and feeling uncomfortable and dissatisfied with his own
conduct during the last month, he hailed one
of those picturesque pleasure boats, anchored
off the Piazetta. It was a fine cool day, not

cloudless, and the wind from the north blowing fresh.

Always partial to the sea, the Marchese felt his mind relieved of a weight, as, taking the tiller, he guided the light bark over the mimic waves of the Lagune, and looked at her tall lateen yard as it bent gracefully at times to the strong squalls.

" It will blow hard before night," said one of the men as they approached the side. " I see the small craft beating up for anchorage ; and the sea birds are coming in in flocks to the sheltered waters of the Lagune."

The wind did rapidly increase, so much so as to require a reduction of canvas ; and then the Marchese, having enjoyed the sail, turned the boat's head homewards.

As they were crossing the deep water of the broad canal leading to Malghera, a fierce squall struck the boat ; but the Marchese had seen it coming, tossing the light spray of the short waves into the air like snowdrift, and the

squall, by skilful management, did no harm.
But one of the men called out—

"Ah! Santa Madonna, Signore, there goes
that handsome barge; the sail jibbed, and she
has gone over."

The Marchese saw the craft go over, and,
slacking sheet, bore down upon her. As they
came near, he could see three persons cling-
ing to the bottom of the boat, which had
turned over, and a few yards from it the body
of a female struggling in the rough water.
Giving the tiller to one of the men, he said—

"Trail your sail," shooting the boat up into
the wind as he spoke. "We are going too
fast to save that female; I can keep her up till
you rescue us," and throwing off his vest and
boots he leaped into the water, and in a few
moments reached the female, who with wonderful presence of mind—for she had not become
insensible—did not grasp at the Marchese as
he came up.

Even in that moment of excitement the

Marchese recognised that young and lovely face as he placed his arm and raised her head above the breaking short sea, and said—

"Have good heart. I will save you with God's help."

A bold and powerful swimmer, it was no feat for the young Marchese to keep her up till the men had trailed their sail, and dropped gently down on them with their oars.

"Oh! Signore, save the others. Oh! Madonna, they will perish!" exclaimed the young girl, as she was lifted into the boat, for not for an instant did she lose her senses; and she could see plainly enough those on the barge struggling to keep their hold.

"Thank God!" exclaimed Ferdinando d'Obizzi, with delight in his glance, as he gazed with wonder at the beautiful being he had saved.

She reclined, much exhausted, upon the low deck of the boat, her luxuriant hair hanging disordered over her shoulders, while the Marchese threw his mantle over her person.

The two men pulled towards the barge, and extricated two men and a middle-aged woman, the latter evidently an attendant upon the maiden the Marchese had rescued. She, however, was insensible, for the two boatmen, neither of whom could swim, had with difficulty maintained their own situation, and held her up.

"Oh! Mariana," exclaimed the maiden, raising her head; "oh! Madonna! I fear she is dead!"

"Oh, no, dear lady," said the Marchese, "she is not dead. Hoist your sail, men, and bear away for Venice."

"Pardon me, Signore," said the young girl, "not for Venice; my mother would be distracted; besides it is nearer to Malghera. We live close to the bank of the river—Casa Bellevista—I daresay the men know the little villa well."

"Yes, Signora, we do," said one of the men; "less than an hour will take us there."

The boat's head was turned for the channel

leading to Malghera, the two boatmen anxiously looking out for a fishing boat in order to go back and take their barge in tow.

Wrapped in all the dry covering the Marchese could procure, the young girl exerted herself to assist the Marchese to recover the attendant Mariana, who soon showed symptoms of returning consciousness. She was evidently a woman of a superior class than the generality of domestics, probably a kind of governess. Nothing could exceed the joy of the young girl, when she saw Mariana open her eyes and look round like one awaking from a deep sleep. She soon recognised the fair girl kneeling at her feet, and, throwing her arms round her neck, burst into a flood of tears.

"There is a boat we know," said the two men the Marchese had rescued; "we will, Signore, if you please, get into her and return to seek our barge luffing up in the wind."

They hailed the skiff, and, getting into her made back for the spot where they expected to find the upset boat.

The young maiden's attendant was soon recovered sufficiently to sit up, and in a very short time the boat ran up the channel, and then entered the small river leading to Malghera, on whose banks was situated the Villa Bellevista.

"There is the villa," said the young girl turning her lustrous bright eyes upon the Marchese, who was attentively sheltering her from the cold sharp breeze, from which he dreaded she would suffer in her dripping, soaked garments. "Ah! Signore," she continued, in her sweet youthful voice, " how can I ever repay the service you have so nobly performed. How little could I imagine, when first we met in the Ducal Palace, that you were destined to be my preserver from a watery grave, and thus save my beloved mother from bitter, unavailing sorrow."

"Then you remember me, dear lady," said the Marchese, with a delighted smile he did not seek to hide. " Your doing so rewards me a thousand times."

"Surely, if you remembered me," she replied, casting down those dangerous eyes, "it
was but natural that I should not forget your
features, though I did not hear your name
mentioned."

"Such was my misfortune," returned the
Marchese, as the boat ran alongside a kind of
quay. "The Duchess left you to my care, but
allowed me to remain ignorant of the name by
which to distinguish you, dear lady, at the
supper."

"My name, in truth," said the young girl,
"was not one of much consequence amid the
noble personages who filled the Ducal saloon
that night. Nevertheless, Justina Coralli will
never forget this day."

The boat was now made fast to the quay,
and two or three female domestics and an old
man, also a domestic, came down the lawn
from the villa to the landing-place.

The villa was a small but beautifully situated
building, completely hedged in on three sides
by groves of evergreens and gardens.

" We must be the first to breathe the news of
this disaster to my beloved mother," said
Justina, taking the arm of the Marchese, and
covered from head to foot in his mantle, which,
however, he was obliged to keep up from its
height and weight, they proceeded up a neat
gravel walk, cut through the lawn to the
villa, while Mariana followed, giving a long
account of their frightful accident to the
astonished domestics.

As they approached the front of the villa,
the young girl's mother had observed them
from the window, and seen at once, by her
daughter's unusual attire and her leaning on the
arm of a strange gentleman, that something
uncommon had happened, for the hall door
opened, and a lady, with a large wrapper thrown
hastily over her shoulders, came out hurriedly.

Wet and dripping as she was, Justina threw
herself into her mother's arms.

" Oh! dear mother! but for that noble
gentleman we should never again have met in
this life."

The mother turned pale as death, uttering a faint cry of alarm, clasping her daughter to her heart with trembling eagerness.

The Marchese, during those few moments, stood gazing with astonishment on the young and singularly beautiful woman that Justina called mother. Releasing her daughter from her embrace, she consigned her to her attendants, entreating and urging her instantly to change her garments. Justina turned to obey, but ere she disappeared she held out her hand to the Marchese, saying—

" Farewell for the present, Signore. What name shall I remember in my prayers ? "

The Marchese kissed respectfully the small and beautiful hand held out to him, saying—

" Dear lady—Ferdinando d'Obizzi is—"

"Ah ! My God !" exclaimed Justina's mother, staggering back. " What name was that ? Pardon me, Signore," she continued, making a violent effort to recover herself, and leading the way into the hall of the villa, " my

daughter's fearful accident and your timely
assistance have quite bewildered my brain."

Justina had paused on hearing her mother's
exclamation, and looked even paler than
before ; but her attendants drew her gently
onwards, and the Marchese entered the principal saloon of the villa with the maiden's
mother, a little startled by the exclamation
uttered by her when she heard his name.

"I will not keep you, Madam," said the
Marchese, "from your fair daughter—besides
my garments—"

" I am strangely forgetful and incautious,"
interrupted the Signora Coralli ; " pray permit
me to have you shown to an apartment, where
some wine and a good fire will be of service."

" Nay, Signora, I must return to Venice at
once.   Wet garments to me are of slight in-
convenience. A glass of wine I will gladly
take, if for no other purpose than to drink
your fair daughter's health, and to hope that no
evil consequences will follow her sad accident."

"You must think me ungrateful, Signore," said the lady, in a voice of much emotion, "but believe me, having saved the life of my dear child, my only child, you have done me a service that no wealth can repay. No words can ever express my feelings, but it pains me to see you in those dripping garments; I cannot permit you to remain thus, and endanger your health. Pray allow me to offer you others till your own are dried."

The old butler just then entered with wine, of which the Marchese drained a full goblet, and then said—

"I must bid you farewell, lady; but will so far presume as to request the permission to visit you another time. Your daughter and I met at the Ducal Palace the day before yesterday. I little thought what was to follow in so short a time."

"We shall, in truth, be most happy to see you—but—" hesitating a little, she continued, "you will oblige me by not mentioning our names to your friends in Venice." Saying so,

she held out her hand, which the Marchese
respectfully saluted, and, bidding her farewell,
hastened to his boat ; and getting aboard was
soon under weigh, and only reached Venice at
sunset, paying the boatmen a princely recom-
pense for their services. He then entered a
gondola and returned to his hotel. Covered
by his mantle, his soaked garments were not
noticed ; and thus he avoided for a time any
needless enquiries as to his strange condition.

CHAPTER XIV.

THE Marchese d'Obizzi awoke the morning after his adventure on the ˋLagune, where he had the happiness of rescuing the object of his waking and dreaming thoughts from a watery grave, in a frame of mind not easily described.   There is no mistaking the love that springs pure and uncontaminated from the heart; it can never be confounded with that love that springs from vanity, selfishness, ambition, or any of the other numerous causes for this holy feeling in the human breast.

With Bianca Grimani he was a little dazzled, and a trifle flattered and gratified by the evident attention she showed him.   She was the first really beautiful and accomplished woman with whom he had ever associated in domestic life.   But his feeling for the lawyer's daughter soon wore out.   He was too young,

and she too much of a woman of the world to
hold long captive so young and romantic a
disposition as Ferdinando d'Obizzi's.

In gratifying himself he had acted wrong;
he had raised hopes and feelings he found had
no place in his own heart; he had considered
her fair name unblemished, but now the case
was greatly altered; though only guilty of
indiscretion, yet her reputation in the eyes of
the world was, to a certain extent, ruined.
Their connection was, therefore, for ever at an
end.

And yet what right had he to love, with a
vow unfulfilled which might render him, if
fulfilled, a wanderer and an outcast. It is true
he might yet find this Duke of Malamocco,
and force him to meet him in honourable fight,
and thus avoid crime and reproach; but the
chances were against him. Was it, therefore,
right, just, or even honourable, with the knowledge of all these drawbacks, to indulge his
passion? Was it right, then, to seek and win
the love of the innocent and lovely girl he had

rescued from death? These and many other thoughts and reflections tormented the mind of the Marchese on the morning after his adventure.

We do not attempt to paint, at the age of twenty-two, a character fixed and determined in its purpose. Ferdinando made an effort to struggle against his heart's wishes, but it was a vain one. He made many honourable resolutions, but he broke them. With the knowledge of that rash and unholy vow in his heart, he yet dared to dream of the love of the pure and spotless heart that dwelt within the breast of Justina Coralli. But there young love had already made his nest, though the maiden herself was quite unconscious of his insidious intentions.

We know not, sometimes, how the blind urchin creeps into our hearts; perhaps a single glance may do the work of months. Certain it is that in the Sunny South, in the balmy air of that favoured land, love is of very quick growth, and when fast-rooted, not to be torn out roughly and at will. In the breast of the Italian, love is the all-powerful feeling; it rules and governs every action; alas! too often giving rise to baleful passion, and in the end destroying body and soul. In the rapture of this new feeling, that was gaining possession of his heart, Ferdinando d'Obizzi did forget for a time the vow that held him in bondage.

The morning following the rescue of Justina from a watery grave, the Marchese d'Obizzi sat by the couch of the Count St. Felix; the fever had in some degree subsided, and the surgeon declared the inflammation much less.

"I shall get up by-and-bye," said the Count to the Marchese. "These men of the lancet make a vast parade in curing a simple thrust of a sword, and I hope this evening you will favour me with your company; and I trust that, notwithstanding the past, when you hear my explanation, you will forgive my certainly cruel conduct, and grant me your friendship, which I shall feel deeply honoured in possessing."

The Marchese pressed the Count's hand kindly; he could not but admire the handsome, prepossessing countenance of the Frenchman, and promising to spend the evening together, he departed.

Taking his own gondola, as the day was fine, and the breeze favourable, he steered for the shore of Malghera, in order to pay a visit at the Villa Bellevista, and enquire for the health of the fair Justina after her watery immersion.

Venice, that strangest of all the cities of Europe, that vast assemblage of magnificent palaces, of gorgeous churches and temples; its towers and campaniles rising against the deep blue sky, the quiet waters encircling it on every side, winding in a hundred strange turnings amidst its buildings; its myriads of boats, of all sizes and shapes; its monstrous galleys and ships of all kinds, scattered over its waters; all had a singular and extraordinary appearance to the eye of the stranger, and to Ferdinando it was yet strange. Though Venice had then

neither gardens nor trees, nor verdure of any
sort to relieve the eye, yet the shores and
islands of the Lagune boasted of much and
varied beauty.

As they entered the channel to Malghera,
the view of the coast before them was lovely,
scattered over, as it was, by the villas of the
Venetian nobles, who lavished thousands on
their gardens, and terraces, and evergreen
groves, composed of the most beautiful shrubs
and trees the climate of Venice could bring to
perfection. Entering the river, the villas
became lost, and the country more open and
less built upon. The villa of the Signora
Coralli, though more retired and secluded, was
still elegant, and beautifully situated on a gentle
rising ground, commanding a fine view over
the wide Lagune, even to the Lido.

That there was some mystery connected with
the mention of his name, the Marchese felt
convinced, for he had painfully observed the
agitation and the start the Signora Coralli had
evinced on hearing it mentioned. She had also

turned very pale, and though she recovered her composure, it was, nevertheless, too apparent.

Leaving his gondoliers to amuse themselves as they pleased during his absence, the said amusement generally consisting of a siesta under the awning, Ferdinando walked up the avenue to the villa. Before reaching the door, he perceived, to his great delight, mother and daughter, arm-in-arm, coming to meet him from a shrubbery at the side of the villa. There was no mistaking the delighted smile that beamed in the beautiful eyes of Justina, as she stretched forth her hand to the preserver of her life; and had the fond mother looked into the eyes of the youthful pair, she could have as plainly read the secrets of their hearts, as if written on an unsullied page. Whether she did or not, we cannot say; but she welcomed the Marchese in a manner that banished all feelings of restraint and fear from his breast.

"I expected you, Marchese," said the mother, " for having given us your name, such *I* know

must be your title. I saw your boat making
up our river; and now you are here, you must
dine with us. The weather is fine, and you
can go back in the evening. I shall take no
excuse, and shall send my old factotum down
for your gondoliers to come up for refresh-
ment. So excuse me for a moment. I have
one little sentence to say to you, that will
insure me your company," and her voice
became low and almost tremulous with emotion,
and as she spoke, she placed her hand upon
his arm, and looked up into his face, saying—

"Ellena d'Obizzi and I were bosom friends
from our earliest years."

At the name of his mother the blood forsook
his cheek, and his strong frame shook; for
conjured up, as if by the wand of an enchanter,
came the vision of his dead grandmother, her
chamber, the picture of his mother, the
portrait of her destroyer, his vow; all rose
before his mind's eye in one picture of the past,
bringing with it agony and remorse.

The young man staggered back, gazing as

if upon reality, while Justina, seeing his sudden paleness and agitation, trembled with some unknown feeling of dread; but, with a strong effort, Ferdinando regained his presence of mind, as the Signora Coralli startled, saying, with the tears in her eyes—

"I have been very inconsiderate. Alas! I forgot that even years cannot obliterate the memory of the past, even in the mind of youth. Will you pardon me, Marchese, for I can say in my heart, if one being ever loved another, I loved your mother."

" Forgive you, madam," returned the Marchese, taking a hand as fair and as beautiful as her daughter's—for Justina's mother more resembled her sister than her mother, so young did she still look, and so graceful and lovely was her person and features.

"'Tis you must forgive my giving way to such emotion on so slight a cause," said d'Obizzi, " but when you mentioned my dear mother's name, a strange and terrible feeling came over my heart. If the saving your daughter's life was before to me an exquisite pleasure, it has tenfold increased, knowing now that the friend of that mother, so revered and adored, is before me."

" Some other time, Marchese, we will talk more of this," said the Signora Coralli.

Justina, while the Marchese spoke, hardly breathed. She had witnessed the terrible change that came over his features, the look of intense agony that rested upon them, and the agitation of his whole frame with fear and anxiety. She knew nothing of the Marchese's history, or of his ill-fated mother's. Her mother had merely said the previous evening, while seated beside her couch, that her pre-server was a nobleman of high and unblemished descent, of immense property, and that his mother was once a dear friend of hers, but nothing more. Left alone with Justina, they walked side by side through the evergreens that bordered the walks, Justina, with her eyes bent upon the ground, wondering in her heart what terrible recollection it could be that had banished so suddenly the smiles and cheerfulness from the handsome face of her preserver.

"It was a very providential thing," said the Marchese, banishing with a sudden effort his gloomy thoughts, "that you have not suffered any cold or bad consequences from yesterday's misfortune."

"It is indeed," was the rejoinder, "but I am not very susceptible of cold, having always been reared hardy. It was singularly providential your boat being near us, for there was no other within a mile or more."

"You were coming from Venice, were you not?" questioned the Marchese, venturing to let his eyes rest on the fascinating and animated features of Justina.

"Yes," she replied, "I had been staying the last few days with the Duchess's youngest daughter. We were four years together finishing our education in the Convent of Santa Madalena, and were bosom friends. She insisted, much against my will, that I should join the supper party at the Ducal

Banquet. I consented, provided the Duchess
did not introduce me to any one of the Venetian nobles, for I am very young and very
timid; and yet, you know, the Duchess,"
added Justina, with a smile, " did not keep her
promise."

"To a certain extent she did," said the
Marchese; " for I have been so short a time
in Venice, and so little known to any one there,
that she thought, probably, my inexperience
was a match for your timidity."

" Where have you been living?" enquired
Justina, with all the innocence and naïveté of
extreme youth.

Seventeen and twenty-two in the opposite
sexes soon drop all the rigid, stately decorum
and distance acquired by years and admixture
with the world.   In less than half-an-hour the
youthful pair, as they sauntered through the
walks of a beautiful garden, became as familiar
and unreserved in their conversation as months
of acquaintance in after years would have
warranted.

Ferdinando told the beautiful girl by his side how his early years were passed far from Venice. He spoke of his service in the Genoese Navy; told her of various services in the far East, that won her eager attention; and when her mother joined them some time after, Justina thought the hour that had passed was the pleasantest and the brightest her young life had yet experienced.

The Signora Coralli was a widow and in years not yet thirty-eight—perhaps a year or two younger than his own mother would have been had she lived.

For another half-hour the three rambled through the small but tastefully arranged grounds of the villa in pleasant conversation, mother and daughter, so young and so beautiful, walking on each side. The past was not then touched upon, for the Signora evidently avoided any allusion to it. The hours flew swiftly by, each pleased with the other, and an involuntary sigh escaped the lips of the Marchese as he arose to depart, after a slight but elegant repast, saying—

" The sun is sinking, dear ladies, on the waters of the Lagune, and I have a sick friend whose couch I promised to visit this evening."

" To the preserver of my child, I need not say," observed the Signora Coralli, " that we shall always be delighted to see him while we remain here ; but in truth, how long that may be, we know not."

Ferdinando felt a chill at his heart, and involuntarily his eyes sought those of Justina. What he read there we can only imagine ; but whatever he did read in those lustrous and speaking eyes, it sank deep into his heart with a thrill of joy.

Kissing the hand the Signora held out to him, he bade her farewell, saying it would not be long before he would avail himself of her kind invitation.   If the small hand of Justina trembled in his, and he slightly pressed it, what can we say, only that young love in young hearts will not always be restrained within the limits of prudence.

Three hours later, Ferdinando d'Obizzi sat with the Count St. Felix in the latter's chamber. The Count reclined upon an ottoman, and on a table near him were several flasks of rich wine, and the beautiful crystal goblets of Venice, not that the Count did more than touch the wine with his lips as he proceeded with his narration as follows :—

" My father, Count Horace St. Felix, was a nobleman of considerable fortune, and held a high place of trust under the Duke of Rohan. He was a·Huguenot, and took an active part in that war against Cardinal Richelieu. I was then a mere child, and resided with my mother and a maiden aunt in our Castle in Languedoc. My father's brother, the Chevalier St. Felix was a Catholic, and served in the army led by Richelieu in person, in Languedoc.

" The Duke of Rohan defended himself with vigour in Languedoc. Nevertheless a party surprised our chateau, and burned it to

the ground. My mother escaped with me
with the greatest difficulty, while my unfortunate aunt perished in the ruins, and the whole
of our property was overrun and laid waste,
and the hand that did this was no other than
my uncle, the Chevalier St. Felix. He hoped
to have destroyed my mother and myself.
We, however, reached Dijon in safety, though
my poor mother caught a severe fever and
cold that ultimately deprived her of life.

"In the meantime, deserted by England,
which had concluded a treaty of peace with
Spain and France, the Duke was forced to
come to a negotiation, and concluded a rather
advantageous peace. But alas! my poor
father did not live to reap the benefit of it, for
a chance shot in a last skirmish deprived him
of life.

"My dear mother bore this terrible blow
with pious resignation, and proceeded to Paris
to claim my father s estates on my behalf; but
my detestable uncle plunged her into a long
and ruinous lawsuit, in the midst of which,

poor soul, she died. I was then but seven
years old, and was confided by my mother to
the care of a maternal relative, a French
gentleman of moderate fortune, but with a very
kind heart. He was a bachelor. Unfortunately
he had neither the means, the interest, nor the
energy to push forward my claims; consequently they vanished, and my uncle finally
took possession of them.

" I grew up into years, with but little knowledge of my parents and less of my rights; for
Monsieur d'Alembert, imagining I had not the
slightest chance of succeeding against the
great interest and fortune of the Marquis St.
Felix—for he had acquired that title through
the interest and favour of Richelieu—left me
ignorant of my claims.

" At the age of eighteen, Monsieur d'Alembert procured me a commission in the army,
and for three years I served in the army of
Louis, who crossed the Alps at the head of
thirty thousand men; gained great advantages
over the Spaniards and Imperialists, and drove

the Duke of Savoy from his dominions. I
rose to the rank of a Captain in a famous
cavalry regiment, and being severely wounded,
went back into France, and finally, with a
brother officer, proceeded to Paris, the war
being at an end.

"My kind relative, Monsieur d'Alembert,
was dead, and left me his entire little patrimony.
I regret to say I now led a somewhat dissipated life, became addicted to pleasure, but
certainly not in the least inclined to seek
fortune at the gaming table. A chance circumstance introduced me to the Marquis de
——, afterwards appointed Ambassador to the
Venetian Republic. He was well acquainted
with my family, and advised me by all means to
put in my claims for my father's estates. My
uncle was then in Germany on a political
mission. I consulted a very eminent lawyer,
put him in possession of my small means, and
he undertook the cause. In the interim I
agreed to accompany the Marquis de —— to
Venice.

"In this gay and dissipated city I led a
rather free life; became acquainted with Captain Grimani, and was by him introduced into
the house of his father. Bianca Grimani was at
this time only sixteen years of age. It will be
quite sufficient for me to say I, at first, only
trifled with her affection, but in the end I
loved her. Bantered by my gay and titled
acquaintances at refusing the love and fortune of a
titled dame of both youth and beauty, but rather
exceptional morals, for a lawyer's daughter,
in an evil hour, and prompted by vanity—for
which God forgive me, for I repented it sorely
since—I persuaded Bianca Grimani to fly with
me to Padua. Captain Grimani with two companions pursued and overtook us, owing to an
accident on the road from Fusina to Padua.

"I could easily have slain Captain Grimani,
but, in pity to his sister, I merely disarmed
him, and whilst bending over the terrified Bianca,
he thrust his sword through my back. I fell
senseless on the bank, and should doubtless
have perished, for he and his companions

carried off Bianca, leaving me to the care of
my only attendant, a young countryman who
was much attached to me, and who, poor
fellow, is since dead. He sought assistance,
and had me carried to a cottage near, and from
thence to Padua. There I remained upon a
sick couch for upwards of four months.

"On my recovery, my intention was to
return and punish worthy Captain Grimani,
who, I must say, is a most unprincipled
young man; but I received letters from
Paris announcing the death of the Marquis
St. Felix, and requesting my immediate return,
for my lawyer claimed the St. Felix estates
in my name, though the title and the other
property went to his eldest son.

"As soon as I was able I went to Paris.
Nevertheless three whole years were taken up
in litigation; but finally I gained my cause
and the restoration of my father's estates.
During the passage of those three years my
mind and disposition were much changed. The
four months also that I spent on a sick couch

effected a great change in my thoughts and
inclinations. I could not but confess that I
had treated Bianca Grimani ill, and as soon as
I settled my affairs I resolved to return to
Venice, and if I found her unchanged in her
affection for me, and otherwise unaltered, I
resolved to repair the injury I must have
inflicted on her reputation, by offering to share
my rank and fortune with her.

" I entered Venice *incognito*, and took up my
abode in the Aquilla Nero, determined to gain
some information as to how matters stood, and
how Bianca had acted during the three years
of my absence.

"In a city like Venice, thanks to dominos
and masks, you may move about as secretly as
you please. You may imagine my vexation
when I learned that Bianca Grimani, so far
from grieving after my supposed death, had
openly declared that I deserved my fate—
perhaps I did—nevertheless I felt piqued;
when I also found out that she not only
encouraged a French adventurer, as a lover,

but on your arrival here, changed her battery, and thought you the better catch of the two, I was disgusted, and after playing the spy for some time, I thought it a pity that you, Marchese d'Obizzi, whom I saw often, and—I beg you to take it as I mean it—prepossessed in your favour by your distinguished appearance and generosity of character, I came to the resolution of saving you from a union in which you never could be happy, the moment you discovered the error she had committed.

" Living in the same hotel with you, I easily watched your movements; saw your blue and silver domino lying on the table; procured another similar, and went to the masked ball to warn you against Bianca. I somehow greatly regret my conduct that night; for after all, Bianca Grimani has not a bad or ungenerous disposition. Too early initiated, amid a bad class of Venetian society, she imbibed some of the bad seed so profusely scattered in her path. I had just met Bianca, and in a moment of pique disclosed myself to her. I had no sooner done so, than I regretted it. She fainted; but seeing her well taken care of, I went in search of you. What passed between us, it is needless to repeat. Your words stung me to the quick, and to pain you, as well as separate you from Bianca, I said she was very 'light of love,' which was false.

"The next day I dropped my *incognito*, and called on young Contarini, with whom I was formerly very intimate—and now I wish to ask you a question—'Is there any cause of enmity between yourself and young Contarini?'"

"None whatever," said the Marchese, in reply, rather surprised. " I never exchanged a dozen words with him since my arrival in Venice."

" Strange ! Very strange," continued Count St. Felix. "I shall certainly request of him an explanation of the words he made use of that night."

"What were they, Count?" demanded d'Obizzi.

" Well, as I trust you and I shall be firm

friends for the future, I will tell you. Contarini
said to me, 'You are the best swordsman in
Venice, St. Felix. Now, if you slay your
antagonist to-night, you will be doing me a
great service.' This he said with a kind of
laugh. 'What do you mean?' I enquired,
rather annoyed. 'Pooh! you are taking my
words seriously,' returned Contarini, with a
sort of sneer I did not like. But we had now
arrived at the appointed place, so I said no
more. Still the words appear strange to me,
and must be explained better hereafter. But
to continue, or rather finish, with the few words
I have to say. Candidly, then, do you love
Bianca Grimani?"

The Marchese coloured to the very temples,
as he replied—

"You may think, Count, and I fear you
will, that my conduct has been not without a
great display of weakness. I was not, neither
am I, in love with Bianca Grimani. I allowed
myself to be pleased, and I frequented her
society more than I was justified in doing as

a mere acquaintance. But I never, upon my honour, spoke of love to her, and in love with her I am not."

" Well, I thought as much myself," returned the Count, thoughtfully. "Still I do not feel satisfied with myself for my conduct to Bianca. That I might have loved her there is no doubt, but a thorough knowledge of her weakness of character, though actually generous and kind-hearted, has destroyed the feeling I once had for her. Besides, I must blame her for the liberty and license she allowed to that rascal, the false Baron de Chatcaunœuf. I wish I had seen that rascal, for, somehow, by the description of him, I fancy I must have met the fellow somewhere. I will write a letter to Bianca, and implore her forgiveness of my sad conduct; renew our intimacy—even if she were willing—(and I know she has too much pride to listen to any proposal of the kind) is out of the question now. As to my duel with her brother, I know him too well; he is not a man of war, though a soldier. Let him cool;

he is fond of bravado; and the days of
butchering one another with poignards are gone
by. I now feel a little fatigued, my dear
Marchese," and, holding out his hand, St. Felix
ended his narrative, by hoping that he should,
from that day forward, look upon the Marchese
as a dear friend.

Ferdinando d'Obizzi pressed the Count's
hand warmly, saying, he felt rejoiced at having
at last found one for whom he could feel a
strong friendship, and to whom he could un-
burden his mind, and, with mutual expressions
of friendship, they separated.

END OF VOL. I.